A Taste of Ecuado

The Collected Stories of Eugenia Viteri

By Eugenia Viteri

Translated by LS Thomas

∞

Jane Knows Intellectual Property, Inc.
San Francisco

English Translation Copyright © 2008 by LS Thomas
All rights reserved.

No part of this publication may be reproduced, stored in a retrieval system, distributed, or transmitted in any form or by any means, including photocopying, recording, or other electronic or mechanical methods, without the prior written permission of the publisher, except in the case of brief quotations embodied in critical reviews and certain other noncommercial uses permitted by copyright law. For permission requests write to the publisher, addressed, "Attention: Permissions Coordinator," at the address below.

Jane Knows Intellectual Property, Inc.
P.O. Box 190142
San Francisco, CA 94119-0142

Publisher's Cataloging-in-Publication
Compliments of Quality Books, Inc.

   Viteri, Eugenia.
     [Short stories. English]
     A taste of Ecuador : the collected short stories of
  Eugenia Viteri / Eugenia Viteri ; translated by LS
  Thomas. -- 1st ed.
     p. cm.
     "Originally published in Spanish as El anillo y otros
  cuentos, 1955 and Cuentos escogidos, 1983"--T.p. verso.
    LCCN 2012931026
    ISBN 9780983146643

   1. Short stories, Ecuadorian.   I. Thomas, L. S.
  II. Title.

  PQ8219.V57A6 2012   863'.64
                           QBI12-600032

First Edition 2012

ISBN 9780983146643
Library of Congress Control Number: 2012931026
Originally published in Spanish as El anillo y otros cuentos, 1955 and Cuentos escogidos, 1983

Manufactured in the United States of America

14 13 12 11 10 9 8 7 6 5 4 3 2 1

To Pedro Jorge Vera, my companion on the road and a friend dear to my heart.

Table of Contents

THE RING 7

MOTHERHOOD 11

A GOOD JOB 13

MINIMA 18

A GREAT BULLFIGHTER 22

THE HEIR 26

THE TRADE 33

MY FRIEND AGUSTIN 40

KID 44

MEN DON'T LIE 48

A PRESENT FOR JACINTA 52

LIFE AND MEMORIES 57

A ROOM FOR RENT 62

FOR CHRISTMAS 67

FRIENDS 71

SHOES AND DREAMS 75

THE DREAMER 82

THE RIBBON TOURNAMENT 88

THE ENCHANTED POTS 92

FLORENCIA	97
THE COFFIN	101
THE WAKE	106
THE EXALTED	110
DOÑA LUCY	113
AN EBONY NIGHT	117
PACHOCHA	122
NEW LILIANAS	125
THE TREASURE	129
THE SECRET	135
PROFESSIONAL CONSCIENCE	139
THE GHOST	143
JACINTO	146

THE RING

Every day, especially on Sundays during the late afternoon, Teresa strolls along the wide beach, called The Liberty. Hunting around, her vivacious eyes scan the distance, and suddenly they alight upon a sunglass case, a fork, a comb: whatever objects are left lying around, forgotten by the swimmers from the city. At times she engages in a real battle with the rough waves to stop them from snatching her prize. If the waves triumph, she sits down on the wet sand and fixes her sad eyes on the sea.

She walks slowly, with her head bowed, her active eyes roving over the sand. Her bright figure does not hold much enchantment, and her walks attract no one's attention. But she only walks for Luis.

She walks for him because the hunt for lost objects is her way of contributing to their subsistence, in order to "help him with something", as she mentioned to him when she saw his salary was insufficient. She did not tell him, but she was also hoping her courage would make him change. But no, he would not change, because the maltreatment he inflicted on her seemed to provoke in him a secret pleasure that he prolonged until she fell at his feet begging his forgiveness. Nevertheless, if she had better luck ... until now she has only had the opposite: trinkets of little value.

She thinks, my God, if only I could find something good.

In any case, she is happy helping out, although it is only a few cents. When he hits her, which happens almost daily, she suffers and waits for some rough caresses by way of recompense. After all said and done, he is her husband.

The brilliance reaches her eyes like a flash of lightning. She, being a connoisseur of found objects--is not deceived: there must be something at that spot on the beach. She runs there. She bends down quickly, fearful someone may surprise her.

"Because this is so pretty, I will keep it for myself," she says.

It is a ring inlaid with brilliant stones which seem to open luminous wings to the sun. Frightened that the waves or the wind will seize it, Teresa cradles it within her tiny hands as if it were alive. Making little hops like a small injured bird, she holds it away from herself murmuring, "It's a real ring, a real ring."

Suddenly, she truncates her joy. Would this time be like the others?

He will say, "Let's see. What did you find? Give it to me."

And, when I give him the object, he'll say, "Junk ...this has no value." And then he will add two or three slaps.

But she returns to looking at the ring. *Ah, no. This, yes, this is good. This one, yes, this one, yes ... and he will go out to sell it for a few cents.*

She would not give it up, not for that. *It is so beautiful!* She tries it on each of her hands one at a time and discovers new facets. It is as if it is many rings in one.

She will not give it up. No. She will keep it only for herself, like a companion for her heart. All alone, she puts it on her finger and it feels secure. She will see everything beautifully in the little mirror disguised within the central stone of the jewel.

Will your mistress be beautiful? And my hands, how will my hands be? They are the white of the well-protected, slow because you do not have to hurry in the middle of your happy life, a life of fulfillment. Ah, my hands are going to glow so much now. I am exonerated by the divine little stones.

Luis stands up when he sees her enter. "And? Do you have something?"

She timidly delays the reply. "Nothing, nothing. This time, I have nothing."

"Hmmm ... How odd, since it's Sunday."

He does not hit her. Perhaps he is very tired; perhaps he perceives a strange courage in her. He shrugs his shoulders and continues dozing.

But the next day, the violent scenes return. Except, to her they no longer seem to matter, since she has her moments of triumph when she is alone; when she gratifies the vanity of an obscure woman and illuminates the feeble soul of an ugly little girl by adorning her hand with the beloved ring. Something makes Luis take note of her, because after scorning her trinkets and hurling curses, he stays his hand which is about to hit her face.

"Your hair looks pretty, you keep looking nice."

She had her hair done in homage to the ring, to the sacred ring that is changing everything. And he has been observing it and observing her face, which is resplendent with a radiance that also comes from the sacred stones in the ring. Then he kisses and caresses her without the usual beating beforehand.

The next afternoon, he returns unexpectedly and surprises her as she stands by the door with her hand extended in silent adoration of the ring.

"What's that? That's nice. Did you find it today?"

She hides her hand behind her back.

"No. No, I did not find it," she says impulsively.

"Then what? Did you steal it?"

"No! No ... they gave it to me."

Luis bursts out in raucous laughter. "They-gave-it-to-me ...! Who would give you a ring?"

Teresa straightens. The words which leave her lips are a lie, a protest for her offended dignity. "A man ... a man..."

Luis' face wrinkles into a frown. He clenches his fists. Teresa closes her eyes and waits for the punches. But Luis does not hit her; he stops, confronted by the strange radiance on her face. He turns around and leaves the room.

After a few minutes, he returns. "Listen. Is this because you want to annoy me? Where did you get that ring?"

"A man gave it to me."

"What man?" he retorts in a furious voice.

"A brown-haired man ... tall with black hair … a man. He says he loves me..." Now she is no longer thinking about her words; they are welling up spontaneously from the dream she has been living. "He wants to carry me away. He calls me: 'My little girl, my beloved.'"

"You idiot! He's going to see..."

Again he closes his fists in order to strike her, and again he remains paralyzed before that face, which is as serene as a lake.

She smiles gently.

"You can't do that. He is waiting for me far away. I will find him soon."

Luis upsets her contemplation with a rictus of anguish. And suddenly it is he who falls sobbing at her feet.

"No, Teresa, you can't leave me. I love you. Return the ring. I will buy you a better one. Today, this very day, I will have them raise my salary."

Teresa gently caresses his bristly hair with her ringed hand. And the ring's stones sparkle like stars in an ebony night.

MOTHERHOOD

Little Pablo lies at the far end of the room. His eyes, rife with fever, want to escape from his swollen eye sockets, while his dry lips whisper, "Mama, come here Mama, Mamaaaaaaa!"

The mother is far away from her son, but through her soul's communion with his, she feels in her own flesh all of the pain which is moment by moment destroying the small frail body of her child.

At night she cannot sleep because she is thinking about her son.

The next day, she confronts her husband with determination. "Eduardo, I have to see my son! I will go today..."

"Be quiet, stupid, you're not going. Don't worry; you'll recover very soon. Or do you want both of you to die? What will you gain by seeing him? What? You'll only transmit it to the newborn baby."

The woman wrings her hands in a painful protest. She knows she is being dominated, and as she presses her lips together, she restrains a moan. It lasts only a second. Suddenly she stands up violently, resolute. But something very tepid slides through her insides and she collapses again: defeated.

She suffers for her son. Her son is crying more from loneliness and neglect than from his sickness.

The hours pass, and the boy with them. After surviving a coughing fit, he is desperate, and with all of his strength, he screams, "Mama, Mama, come now!"

Quick steps sound on the hard floor. When they arrive next to his bed, a sweet voice brings serenity to his agitated soul. "I am here, my son."

"Come closer, Mama. I can't see you anymore. And let me touch your little face ... like this... I want to hold you in my arms. But you're crying, Mama. Why? If I go away to wait in the sky..."

"Son! Quiet, be quiet!"

"Mother, do you want to give me a big kiss, very big?"

"Son, son!"

The cough returns again, and the boy is in mortal anguish. "I'm choking Mama, give me air; give me light...."

He soon calms down, with his weak hands clasped around the neck of the woman whom he believes to be his mother.

In this way, sweet Pablo leaves the world.

The nun's face acquires a beatific expression while her heart overflows with an infinite tenderness for the son, who had never known the sanctuary of her sterile womb; and yet she feels ripe and fertile from having deceived this strange boy.

I have been his mother today. Mother, nonetheless of a dead child.

A GOOD JOB

"Fernando ... my daughters. You look ... look after them ... Fernando ... my daughters."

Only when the voice fades, between alarm and poignancy, does Fernando comprehend the enormous responsibility he has incurred.

Why did I do it? My God, why did I promise him? And what can I offer them? Nothing, if I have nothing. And yet I have promised.

The whole thing began when Fernando was admitted to hospital, a victim of his youth, money and women. The women, who had almost destroyed his very life, had been mainly to blame for his admittance to the hospital.

Yes, it was in the hospital that this all began...

"I'm your neighbor: Fermin Yanez." The sick man extends his hand.

"Friend, my name is Fernando Castro!"

"Look, friend. In the beginning it's difficult to get used to this exile, but with time you end up feeling just like you're at home. One misses the home, the wife, the adorable daughters, but ..."

He couldn't say more. A sob cut his sentence short.

Perhaps it was his kind words, or his serious fatherly face, which makes Fernando feel sympathetic towards this man, who seems very ill. And the bond of their friendship slowly strengthens until it turns into an urgent, unavoidable sentiment.

One afternoon ...

"Fernando."

"Ah?"

"Today, my wife wrote to me. She finally agreed not to come. It hurts me so much that they might know the truth ..."

His grey eyes, full of pain and a faraway look, caress the door through which he would never exit. Then slowly, very slowly, he turns his head and reclines on his pillow. He appears to be very tired and it costs him dearly to speak.

"All right, what's your story?" Fernando asks.

"Ah ... yes. The poor work hard; one does it for the girls ..."

"For the girls, and for you," I say wanting to show I care.

"Yes, you were right when you said 'and for you.' But what good am I to them? I can't end up dying ..."

"Patience, Fermin. Soon you will be well."

"No, I don't want to deceive you too."

His voice had risen until he was shouting, and his fevered body shook beneath the white sheets which would soon serve as his shroud.

Suddenly his voice returns to being as serene as a lake, as distant as an echo. "Fernando, my friend, each day I get worse."

"Don't be a pessimist."

"Be quiet!"

After a while, he continues talking. "Fernando, thank you for everything you've done for me."

"But Fermin...."

"Let me speak. What you have done is great ... very great. In becoming my companion, you pretended to be very sick and you put up with the unpleasant consequences. And only a real friend does that. Now I want to ask you one thing, the last one, Fernando."

His teary, bright eyes were staring; his lips, red from the fever, quiver in supplication, and Fernando strongly squeezes both of Fermin's cold emaciated hands in his own.

Then I couldn't imagine what he was going to ask next. And still, I might have imagined it. How could one say no to those eyes, those lips, those hands?

"Take care of my daughters. They need a man to watch over them and to protect them. See that they don't go hungry; the relatives help and my wife works too. Do you promise it to me, Fernando?"

"Yes, I promise."

"Right, now I can stay calm, I hope. There's one more thing—delay a while before giving them the news, until they get used to you."

A few days later, the empty bed indicated my destiny. I had made a promise, and had to fulfill it.

He is facing the door, but has not yet decided to knock. He seems to hear Fermin's voice: 'Delay a while before giving them the news, until they get used to you.'

He wants to retreat and escape, but Fermin's eyes are always fixed on his.

A woman, with a thoughtful look and a sad smile, comes out to receive him.

"Come in, come in. You're Fermin's friend. He has written about you in his letters. And how is he?"

"Better."

"Better," the woman repeats with a smile. She is intelligent and it is unnecessary for him to say more. Later she calls the girls so they can meet him.

But, if Fermin had suffered in his bed, the girls had grieved at home. They have nothing to eat. The sewing machine, which the mother used for work, has been sold because of the illness. And as for the statement "the relatives' help", it was a lie.

And Fermin had not known.

Fernando, who had considered leaving after visiting them, invites them to go out for a walk instead.

Poor girls. A walk will cheer them up. And they are so small and alone. Alone in the house, and alone in the world. Not alone, no! They are with me and I'm here to defend them.

"Fernando, another day might be better," the mother apologizes.

"Now," chorus the girls gleefully, clapping their small hands. "Now, now!"

As the girls hold Fernando's hands, they make a great discovery.

"Little sister, that yellow car is pretty isn't it?"

"Uh, this one is the best."

"That great big house is mine."

"No mine. I saw it first."

Fernando feels happy. Another man has sprouted up inside him and this new man shows love towards the girls, and happily goes along with them as if he were their father.

It is a long walk, and the hunger confined inside the girls violently unfurls.

"Fernando, a delicious smell is coming from those pretty houses."

"Of course, little sister: it smells like good food."

"Fernando, don't pay attention to them. The girls are a bit thoughtless."

"No, ma'am. It's because it's dinner time."

"Then you'll take us there, Fernando?"

"Yes, I'll take you there."

What am I doing? What am I going to do? I only have two sucres. My God, why didn't I think of that before? And yet the girls must have something to eat.

He settles them in a restaurant and orders a good dinner. The mother remains silent and distant, remembering the times of prosperity with her husband. In contrast, the girls are laughing at everything.

Looking at them, Fernando thinks: Who knows how long they haven't eaten? But they're eating, they're happy and that is what's important.

"Fernando, you seem preoccupied," the mother says suddenly.

"Ah, yes ... This ... I ... I'm thinking about my business ma'am. That is to say... about the business that must be addressed. For this reason, I regret that I can't accompany you to the house. But they may have this money for the bus. I'll come and see them later."

The girls say goodbye with kisses; the mother says it with a grateful smile.

Now alone, he approaches the waiter for the bill. Fernando stutters some words. Without understanding them, the waiter calls in another man, perhaps the owner, who vigorously demands that he pay. Eventually Fernando says the terrible words, "I don't have any money."

Now he receives a chorus of insulting words. There are injuries, but to him they seem very far away, as if they are not for him. *It is not about me; I don't have to respond.*

All of a sudden, he feels himself being thrown like a small spinning top, and then he does not remember anything else.

When he awakes, he is completely soaked and abandoned in an empty lot. He recalls the scene: the man's fists, his furious eyes...

He raises his hands to his face. No, he does not have a broken face; only a black eye. His ribs? They are also intact. But his whole body hurts when he moves.

Who made me get myself into this mess?

Unexpectedly radiant with joy, he stands up, and as he raises his face to the sky, he murmurs, "Fermin, Fermin, now your daughters have something to eat. Today I did a good job."

MINIMA

For want of provisions, the rundown shop is infested with moths and termites. Occasionally, pale children are seen arriving, who between timidity and fright, ask for forty cents worth of rice, or six *reals* worth of lentils, or one *sucre* worth of lard.

Aurelio Arreaga, the owner of 'The Flower of Zapotal', is afflicted with asthma and constantly panting, his small coffee-brown eyes shine with rage, maybe for the necessity of breathing audibly. Perhaps he has waited too long to go on a trip to Guayaquil in search of a kilogram of rice or a box of candles.

He is consoled by the imminent arrival of the International Petroleum Company.

"That day everything will change because those white people are big spenders. And many Guayaquilians will come with them also. Yes, we will make silver."

He spends hours and hours doing projections, calculations and even balancing the books. He advises his wife in a solemn tone, "Yes, in China they know how to run big businesses."

And, heaving a deep sigh, he takes one pencil and exchanges it for the one behind his ear. He wets it in his mouth, and then writes out extensive additions in a dilapidated yellowed notebook.

Only Rebecca, his young daughter, takes no interest in the profitable business, and that makes her father sigh. She is happy just stroking Minima, the small beloved cat with silky molting black fur. After ten years (possibly well-lived), Minima has turned into a sleepyhead and passes every morning and afternoon confused between the potatoes and onions.

Whenever Rebecca goes to find her, the cat slowly and lazily stretches herself. Then she jumps into the lap of her mistress, who leaves at a run carrying her precious cargo.

In this way, simply and without complications, Minima's life glides by until the time arrives for becoming rich. The International Petroleum Company is sending cars and more cars, full of workers who settle in the small village. Things are turning out just how Aurelito had dreamed. The business continues to grow, and grows and grows at a faster rate; so much so, that he is constantly preoccupied with it, to the detriment of his marriage and his daughter. Only Minima remains impassive and happy now atop of numerous kilograms of rice.

One night, the family meets to discuss a change of residence. Now they are rich. After three years of fruitful business, they find themselves in a position to be able to buy a house and build a warehouse where Rebecca's small smooth brown hands could take all the silks, powders and perfumes that she wanted.

This event proves to be a point of contention for the family.

Mr. Arreaga dreams of a voluminous bank book. His wife imagines ruling over several servants and organizing her clothes and jewels. Rebecca catches a glimpse of her blue prince; when she is older, her admirers will no longer be *cholos* from Zapotal.

The next morning, after the move to the new house, Rebecca appears wearing an opulent dress. She looks for the cat.

"Minima, dear," she says to her very happily, "I have great news for you: you are rich, immensely rich. I want to make you look more elegant. I'm going put this collar on you—it's made of the best satin silk—and this silver bell—yes it's pure silver, just like Papa said. Like this, see? How precious you are! You're the most adorable little cat in the world."

Rebecca kisses her tenderly, but Minima neither purrs nor moves her tail.

"My dear, what's happening to you? Ah, right. And the worst of it is that you have a reason. I'm talking and talking, and yet I haven't shown you your room. Let's go, through here...."

She leaves the cat settled in her own room, lying on a cushion made of brilliant red fabric.

But Minima does not purr again. She feels tortured by the nostalgia of those happy days, when strength, cunning and agility had been needed to conquer her daily bread. And then, to think that every afternoon the rats dance and squeak merrily in the granaries of the world. And she is far away, separated from their paths forever. Transported to this strange, unfamiliar environment, nothing reminds her of her tranquil past life. She cannot even frolic for a few moments because the floor is too cold and shiny. If she would only stroke her, what a pleasure it would be. But no, that is not possible; they would tear the silks and ruin the cushions, and her mistress would not forgive her for it.

When she thinks about this new and foreign, strange life—this bell and this collar, the collar that almost strangles her—she feels desperate at not being able to extricate herself from the things which annoy her. Minima leaves, running toward the road. A few boys on the street are attracted by the sound of the bell and chase her while shouting after her. She jumps and jumps, until a well-aimed stone leaves her immobile. The young boys who surround her see a desperate need for help in her eyes. There is so much pain in those eyes that it makes the boys frightened and they leave her alone.

With difficulty, Minima continues as far as the little store which is now dark and abandoned, but so full of those unmistakable smells of potatoes, onions and cabbage that were there when her youth slipped by. She would have ended her life there, had Rebecca not noticed her absence. Rebecca searches all of the rooms in the grand house and does not find the cat. In desperation, she asks her father to let her go and look elsewhere.

"Hummm, I don't miss her at all. You worry too much about a filthy cat, a very cold-hearted cat."

But since the girl continues crying, he lets her go.

Minima is languid and immobile. Her mistress' arms do not succeed in reviving her. Rebecca bursts out crying and screams. Suddenly she understands everything: Minima's sadness, her running away.

She leaves the empty little store and goes to her nearest friend's home. When she returns to Minima's side, a miracle happens: Minima slowly raises her tail. She sniffs her mistress' dress, hands and hair. She moves her head and a faint, barely perceptible sound makes her small neck vibrate, and then she purrs. She would be happy again and forgive her mistress if only, for just one minute, Rebecca could go back to being poor with little old shoes and a percale dress.

"Minima, don't die. Minima, I love you."

Her father, who has followed her, says, "Don't worry daughter. It was a stray cat. I'll give you the silver to buy an angora cat which is the best cat or even a tortoiseshell if I have the silver for it."

A GREAT BULLFIGHTER

Ignacio is barely one year old, and his father already believes he can see his future in the bullring.

"You too will be a bullfighter, my handsome little boy!"

Ignacio smiles, showing his only three teeth. His mother, without raising her eyes from her sewing, feels a reawakening of the anguish which has dominated her life: he in the bullring, applauded by the multitudes; she alone kneeling before the holy image, imploring, 'Blessed Virgin, cover him with your mantle. See that nothing happens to him; see that nothing happens to him.'

Between the tears and caresses of his mother, between the triumphs and songs of his father, Ignacio grows. Neither capes nor banderillas, neither bull's ears nor tails, excite him. His father is getting worried.

"You'll see little son, what a career bull fighting is! Fame, applause, money and women."

His mother looks up and timidly protests. "Leave the boy alone, let him study!" And she closes her eyes, certain of the sweet miracle. Up to that time she has managed to prevent Ignacio from ever going to the bulls, and because of this his tranquil character distances him from the agitated and turbulent world of his father.

His father's triumphal tour of foreign lands lasts for two years. He returns covered in glory to make a new appearance in his home city, and this is a sensational event.

"Listen, Ignacio, does your father fight this afternoon?" one of his friends asks.

He nods.

"Get us in!"

"I don't go."

"Yeah, yeah! Don't get hot, pal. I'm sure he sez he feels sorry for them."

"If I was in your place, I would be proud of a father like that," a third boy points out.

"Well, of course, he's a real bull fighter."

An expression of bitterness grows on Ignacio's face.

"Good, brother, let's go, Ignacio's got his head in the clouds."

"Hey you, we're going to see the bulls this afternoon."

"The what?" Ignacio asks, descending from the clouds.

"The bu-lls. But you don't want to see them ..."

"... because I feel sorry for the bulls," another boy says with a sneer, mimicking Ignacio. And, sticking out his tongue, he leaves at a fast run, together with his companions.

Ignacio hesitates for an instant, and then goes after the three boys. By exerting himself, he manages to catch up with them just as they are arriving at the outskirts of the bullring.

"Look, what terrific bulls!"

"This afternoon is going to be really great."

"Ignacio, don't be an idiot, come see your father triumph. You'll see how he brings down those big bulls."

They are all powerful and magnificent beasts, eager to fight so it seems. But Ignacio is affected by their bitter, almost desperate glances, like defeated athletes waiting for death. And above all, he is impressed by a defiant black bull who bellows in a consummate fury, as if he were begging for love with his sad eyes.

This bull is the portrait of the rebel's pain.

Maybe they won't succeed in killing him this afternoon; maybe my Papa will not have this bull.

"But Ignacio, what's the matter with you?"

"What a sad face!"

Ignacio glares at them with hatred.

"Idiots!" he yells. "You wouldn't be happy if you knew that they're going to kill them."

They respond with raucous laughter. While they leave him behind, he continues to be invaded by melancholy from the enormous black bull.

How sad the poor little thing is! I have to do something to help him, to save him, save him, yes. He must live, he must live.

He finds his mother praying. In a very low voice, so as not to offend the Virgin, he asks her, "Did he leave already?"

"Yes, my little son. But where have you been? Your father has asked me many times to allow him to bring you."

"I'm going by myself. I have to go."

She is displeased with the forceful energy behind his words. She has consented to his father taking him just this once, since she is sure the boy will not be enthusiastic about the bloody entertainment. And now she observes him looking brusque, hard and unyielding—almost like a great bull fighter.

"Blessed Virgin, protect my son too. See that his father doesn't win him over from me. I don't want him to be a bull fighter."

The spectacle does not excite him. The bullfighter plays with the cape, dances, kneels down, and kills. The bull is dragged away while the people applaud.

Now it is his father's turn, when he appears, there is a thunderous ovation. He is met by the furious, melancholy black bull; its neck lowered, its legs tense, its gaze mournful. His father teases it, challenges it, and charges at it. His figure moves swiftly as he opens flowers of blood with his banderillas. And in the midst of the roar of the intoxicated crowd, he sinks his sword into the bull's robust back.

"Stop, Papa, stop! Look at his eyes!"

Ignacio runs crying into the center of the bullring. As if with a single immense chest, the crowd lets out a strident scream. The beast, bloody and watery-eyed lays down at the boy's feet and gives him a docile look. And the jubilant father lifts his son, shouting, "My son is a bullfighter, a great bullfighter!"

THE HEIR

My wife and I are still in the bedroom when someone knocks at the door. Margarita hurries to open it and meets Andres, the kid in charge of delivering groceries to Peter Morris, the English engineer.

Stuttering, he says, "Mr. ... Peter ... is ... dead."

We rush to our friend's home and verify that he is indeed dead. Since Peter lived by himself, it is left to us, his best friends, to make all the arrangements for the funeral. We are busy organizing things when I remember Peter's sister, who lives on a beach where she is the manager of a hotel. Immediately I call Andres and instruct him to send a telegram.

We have finished the work. Out of curiosity I pick up a book from the nightstand. When I open it, a note falls out.

It says, 'Margarita, destroy the package bound with a blue ribbon that you find in the wardrobe.'

I take the package without either Margarita or the maid knowing about it. Then I tell my wife that I am going to fetch the coffin from the mortuary, and I leave. Once I am on the street, I search for a place to open the package. I find a bar and order a double cognac. While they are bringing it, I call a funeral agency, give them directions to the house and return to my table. My anxious fingers rapidly rip off the ribbon and tear open the package. Lying there before me are some letters with the words, 'To My Margarita', written on them.

My face must be turning quite pale because the waiter says, "Sir, is something wrong?"

"No, nothing. Noth-ing!"

But I do not know what the letters say. Why are they addressed to my wife? Maybe she is not the only Margarita in existence.

I begin reading:

Adorable Margarita,

I've spent the whole night with you. My senses opened to perceive you as if you were here by my side. The strength of my passion is so great that it can give substance to your image even when I am alone. On my lips, I taste your kisses; in my hands, I feel the coolness of your flesh; in my eyes, I see your sweet gaze; everything about you is in me.

Forever yours,

P.

My Little Girl,

Today has been a marvelous day for me. I held you in my arms; I kissed your mouth; I drank your blood. What more could one desire?

Your Peter

Dear Little One,

If I had to live life listening only to your words, without ever having you in my arms, without carrying you on my skin, and in my senses, without being the possessor of your blood, then I would have to be thankful for the waves which bring me your pure music and your passionate words. The little white dress you wore last night was divine. The cleavage was very perturbing for me. Do you know why? Because other men were staring at your breasts. How ingenuous! Don't they know that they only spill out for me?

I adore you.

Your Peter.

We have a son, Margarita,

A son who will conquer the oceans, count the stars and sleep on the seashore when he has completed his mission on Earth.
P.

I no longer have any doubts; the woman is Margarita, my wife. I continue reading …

'Our son is one year old, Margarita. He already says, "Papa", and is so fragile and so gentle that sometimes I think that he won't be a sailor. And I think of how much I have suffered because I believed that his life would cost me yours, but by the grace of the god, your precious lives continue, your hearts continue beating with love and happiness for me.'

Yes, now I remember ... everything, yes. She was the one who wanted to call Peter. How my friend suffered when Margarita was subjected to an operation in order to remove the tiny child alive. Such was his anguish that the doctor thought he was the husband. And I believed he was a good friend. Yet he was robbing me of my wife, my son, my love. A good friend ... what a friend…

It is eleven forty-five a.m. By now Peter must be ready to embark on his journey, and I will have time to search through her letters. Margarita is not in the house; the maid says I can find her with the boy at Mr. Peter's house. She is in her son's father's house taking care of him until the final moment, loving his corpse. Suddenly the door opens and I see Margarita enter. There is pain and fatigue on her face.

"Sit down," I say to her, "you need to rest."

"Yes, I am very tired. I was able to come home because Peter's sister has just arrived."

On seeing her eyes so sad, I feel the temptation to kiss her, to press her lips with mine. But, no. Why should I do it if her grief is for the man who has robbed me of so much loving?

The next day, Peter's sister comes to thank us and to execute her brother's will; to deliver the testament to his beneficiary.

"He left everything to your son, Mr. Fernandez."

"To my son?"

"Yes, to your son, my esteemed sir. My brother appreciated all of you a lot. You constantly showed him signs of love and friendship."

Yes, above all Margarita, I struggle to say, but I say nothing.

She thanks us again and leaves.

"Margarita, who is your son's father?"

She looks at me entranced, and after a long silence, she says very tenderly, "What happened to you, my love? Are you sick?"

When she puts her hand on my temple, she discovers that it is burning.

"I understand dear, it's the grief for Peter, plus the surprise just now."

Exasperated, I shout, "I don't see why I'm obliged to feel grief for Peter."

The Heir

"Ernesto! Peter was our friend. You are sick, aren't you?"

"Yes, I am." I withdraw from her side.

Like a rabid dog, salivating bitterness, I go to Peter's house. I meet his sister.

"I've been waiting for you Mr. Fernandez."

"Please don't be anxious, and accept the treasure of Margarita."

"He requested that you surrender her to me?"

"No, but I believe a husband can acquaint himself with letters addressed to his wife; especially if he knows about her affectionate nature."

A diabolical smile grows on that ice cold face. Then she continues, "This letter was sent to me by my brother, together with the will, a few days before he died. The poor man was so romantic, wasn't he?"

This is the worst thing I have heard in my life, worse than Margarita's betrayal, because this woman believes that I am guilty.

My head is dancing my hands are in the way. In the shadowy room, Peter's sister's fine, languid silhouette stands out and transforms into my judge.

"Mr. Fernandez, I invite you to read the letter in order to substantiate my words."

I tear open the envelope without looking at those little accusing eyes, which are screaming, 'Cuckold, cuckold' at me.

Here is what the letter says:

>Margarita, my little one,
>
>You will never know how much I have loved you and that in my dreams you were

my ideal companion, the woman who, in my life of confirmed bachelorhood, I would have longed to have found. Destiny did not wish it, and when our paths crossed, you could not be more than a friend to me. In spite of this, without your knowing, without my ever propositioning you, you conquered my affection. I am grateful to you for the sweet dream that I lived by your side. The reality was far from this; for this reason I poured my passion into these letters, which I wrote without giving them to you. If only I had an alarm clock for my dream, for my enchantment. Being as dignified as you are, you would have rejected them. I only woke up today, when I found myself on the verge of a fall, and I request your forgiveness. Don't curse my name. It is not my fault that I have found in you the woman of my dreams. I sincerely salute my best friend Ernesto. He lavished me with genuine moments of happiness when he offered me a refuge at his hearth, and even made me feel like a father to his tiny tot. I give the child everything I own, and I hope that you three will remember me with affection. Please, destroy those letters Margarita, so that Ernesto won't see them. Men can be awkwardly jealous when we possess a treasure like you.

Good-bye, Peter.

I seem to hear Peter's voice saying the words, 'Men can be awkwardly jealous when we possess a treasure like you.'

Forgive me Peter, Margarita.

Peter's poor sister remains engulfed in her grief, lost in solitude, gnawing her envy.

And I, being as happy as a child with lots of toys, run to find Margarita. I caress her tenderly, and her response is to surrender into my arms fully and completely.

THE TRADE

The walls in the parlor are covered with a black fabric, as is the vaulted ceiling where a rose-colored light hangs. In the distance, sits a round table, and on its top are paper, a pencil and a dog-eared book full of prayers. The chairs are arranged in a closed oval around the table. A little to its left is a small door which provides a salvation in case the medium has to escape.

There are two young women in the room: the first is thin and fragile; the second, by contrast, has wide hips and an overflowing bosom. It is evident that the two of them share a common, deep preoccupation: To tell everything ... to ask for a remedy.... They have been told that there are spirits which perform veritable miracles.

Soon, the parlor fills with a diverse crowd of people, all with desires and problems that momentarily surface in their anxious eyes.

The two women, who have already started talking in low voices, easily form a palisade when the small door open and a pot-bellied man with timid eyes enters walking slowly.

"I'm scared Ernestina! I'm scared!" The thin woman clasps her friend's arm strongly. Even though she is a little frightened, she projects serenity.

"Calm down Cecilia. Look, now the medium is approaching."

The pot-bellied man with sensual lips stops next to the table. Without lifting his gaze, which is fixed on his hands in an attitude of supplication, he greets his clients.

"Peace and health to you, Sisters and Brothers!"

Everyone responds with one voice, "Peace and health to you, Dear Brother!"

The medium continues speaking in a resounding voice, "My Sisters and Brothers, I want you to think about the spirit of Friar Vicente

Solano, the spiritual guide for The Light Psychic Center, while I pray the traditional petition for initiating the session, and ask him to give us his holy benediction."

The attendees stand with their hands held over their hearts and repeat the medium's words in low voices.

"Good spirits, holy spirits found in heaven in the presence of the divine creator. Tell me, our spiritual guide, if you are there this moment in the infinite space. If you are there, may you be permitted to immediately come to us; and inform us by knocking on the table."

The medium, who has remained standing, sits down. At the same time he places his hands on the table. His bowed head and faraway voice indicate that Friar Vicente Solano is present.

"Virtue and peace, dear Sisters and Brothers. I, Friar Vicente Solano, am with you. I allow you to begin a session, and I give you your benediction: in the name of the Father, the Son, and the Holy Spirit, Amen."

Tock! The voice is silenced by a sharp knock.

"Oh, what was that?" the thin, little woman asks one of her neighbors, a tall slightly stooped woman with a prominent nose that stands out from her pale face.

She gazes at her enquirer before responding. "That was dear Brother Solano who is going away. Can't you see that the medium is in a trance?"

"Aaaah, when the big man closes his eyes, it's because he's in a trance?"

"Yes, but be quiet as this is not the time to talk."

The pot-bellied man begins a new fervent prayer: "Spirits who possess the goodness of god, please tell me if you can come before us, Brother Marino Tengle."

Tap ... tap ... tap

No one realizes the three faint knocks the medium makes on the table are to indicate that Brother Tengle was not found free in space.

"Well, Sisters and Brothers, then send me the spirit of Brother Ozara so that he may possess my body, and deign him to come to join the sisters and brothers who are here for various reasons."

He then falls heavily into the chair, his muscles relax and slowly, very slowly he begins to sway.

The crowd remains silent with their eyes riveted on the medium, watching his movements.

At last he stops moving, sits up straight in his chair, and patiently waits for the sisters and brothers to approach him, one by one, to tell him their problems.

The consultations are brief. When they end, a conveniently-located saucer receives the price of the consultation. It is never less than five *sucres*.

The last attendees are the two friends. Although they had arrived first, they prefer to wait. When there is almost no one left, the thin, shaking woman slides up to the table.

"Dear Sister, what is your problem?"

"My husband, Dear Brother... my husband is leaving me for another. I want you to make me a remedy for him so that he will forget her."

"Good Sister, but that is going to cost you a little something. Well, I see that your case is very difficult. However, I assure you that if you so desire, your husband will return to you; he'll return devoted." And he raised his arm very high. "I have never failed, never! I tell you that because I like to warn you. It will cost you, it will cost you. You know, Sister, that the one who wants heaven ..."

"Don't worry about the money, dear Brother. I will pay you what you ask."

"Good, I'm going to give you a prescription, which you must follow to the letter with your feet."

He raises his hands to his hard, slightly-inclined head, adopts a solemn attitude, and orders, "Take a medal of Saint Elena and a picture of your husband. Wrap these two things in a green silk cloth. At the level of your heart, drive in three gilt nails. Then hold a vigil over it for fifteen days and fifteen nights. I guarantee that, at the end of that time, your husband will have returned to you."

"Oh, dear Brother, you have the mouth of an angel! How much do I owe you?"

"For now, only two hundred *sucres*. Afterwards, when you are back with your husband, you can give me the rest."

The woman takes a white envelope form her bosom. She quickly opens it and bows slightly in gratitude to the brother while she places the two bills on the saucer.

It is her friend's turn. The woman with wide hips and an overflowing bosom approaches heavily.

The previous question is heard again. "Dear Sister, what is your problem?"

"Dear Brother, I have a business in the market place. But it is not going well. Sometimes I make a profit and sometimes I don't."

"Ah, Sister! I see that your business has been ailing. They have made it so that you are poor all of the time" Then, smacking his sensual lips, he says, "Your case is serious ... very serious. You will be unhappy if you are not healed! However, you are lucky to have fallen into my hands."

"Yes, dear Brother, yes. Heal me, you heal me. For that, I will pay you until my last *centavo*."

"Good, good. Stand up. First I am going to take some steps to remove the bad influences that they have placed on you, like this you see,like this." His avid hands glide over her from head to calf. He is so deeply involved in his labor that he almost forgets the others. However, at the end of several minutes, he finishes giving the massage.

"Now, sit down and listen to me." The man's face, which moments earlier had been tense and sweaty, takes on a look of serene relaxation. "Take a small pouch made of red silk, put a large clove of garlic, some mint, parsley, sugar and incense in it. Sew it up and take it to seven different churches, and bathe it in holy water at each one of them. When bringing it into your house, pray in this way: 'Sisters and Brothers free me from my enemies who wish wrong on me. Free me, Sisters and Brothers, free me, free me.' With that you are served, Sister. But the work costs three hundred *sucres*."

"Take them, dear Brother, and thank you. Thank you very much."

"You do not have to thank me for it, Sister, since we came to Earth in order to help humanity; the defeated and abused of humanity ..." He is acquiring a solemn tone. "..., that humanity which still struggles with hunger and pain. Where would you be without us? Where would you be, small creatures brutalized by the vile corruption of the flesh which you nourish materially without ever thinking about your spirits and without frequently visiting those places where there is knowledge of morals and wisdom? Here we have our mission: to help you, to guide you when you give us the opportunity."

The woman, who has been listening to him with her mouth open, tries to fully comprehend the immense value of this noble spirit. She thanks him again and goes to join her friend who is still waiting for her. They shake hands and leave content.

Inside, the medium continues sitting in a trance-like state.

"Papa, Papa! Open your eyes. No one is here but me."

The man sighs, yawns widely, and then rubs his eyes with the back of his hands.

"And how was your day, Papa?"

"Ah, yes, it wasn't bad. I had two excellent jobs."

"That's good, Papa, that's good!" The teenager laughs while arranging an unruly lock of his hair.

"Help me count these crickets in groups of five *sucres*," his father orders.

The boy begins counting. "One, two, three, four, five." He pauses, looks at his father, and asks, "Papa, when are you going to teach me the trade?"

The father, who is bending over the table, does not stop counting. "This... First you have to study."

"Study? But why, Papa, why?"

"Because you have to be different."

His father's sharp, furious voice frightens him. He has never seen him so forceful, so severe.

"Son, understand me! You must study, you can't continue in this ... Listen to me and you will never have to feel sorry for yourself."

"But, why don't you feel sorry for yourself then?"

The medium waves his arms in disgust. "My case is different."

"And why isn't mine? Why?" The boy is shouting. "I was born here in the mountains ... here, listening to you exploiting those ... imbeciles every day. And now you want me to be different. Well, no! Your trade will be my trade, the trade of my sons, of my grandsons."

"No! No! It's repugnant! Not this trade! Continue at high school, and then go on to the University. You will be a lawyer; that's an honorable profession."

"A lawyer? Not that, Papa! You want me to be a lawyer, like the attorney next door? That's even worse than this. At least people leave here content. The peasants leave the lawyer's house crying. Like that widow the other day; what a curse! A lawyer, never!"

The boy makes a brusque gesture and leaves.

On the floor, near the father, the wind impatiently leafs through the book full of prayers.

MY FRIEND AGUSTIN

When I met him, he was a chubby, broad-faced man, who was perhaps fifty years old. In spite of his frayed clothes and moribund shoes, neither his voice nor his expression reflected suffering. His eyes were like two little birds cheerfully dancing on the good-natured horizon of his face. His wrinkled lips opened into a permanent smile.

At that time, I was only ten, and I went to the newspaper stand almost daily. That afternoon, I did not have to pay to rent all of my favorites. I was content, well, with just looking through them.

"Hey, little one, would you like to help me?"

I turn around quickly. I help him carry all the books and magazines he displays for sale or for rent. Before we are finished, we are already great friends.

Without thinking about paying me for my work, he invites me to his small house at the far end of our village.

"Sit down. What's your name?"

"Raul."

"Raulito, I'm going to bring you a glass of milk."

This is the beginning of our friendship. So thought provoking, so comforting is his company, that he becomes indispensable to me. We see each other every day at his bookstand, and when there are no customers to attend to, he delivers a picturesque narration, which he illustrates with gestures and poignant postures. I am all ears.

"Well, then … 'The Widow of Tamarind' …"

"No, Agustin, you've already told me that one. Now tell me about your life as a sailor on the steamboat."

My friend is annoyed at the interruption, but he immediately recovers his enthusiasm. For him, the importance is in the telling.

He passes his hand over his face and begins. "Well, when I was on the 'Ana Mercedes'... No, no! It's better for me to describe the most unusual thing that happened to me. You're big enough to hear it now."

He leans back on his stool and starts the tale. "I was eighteen years old and I was all sailor. Boy, what muscles!" He brings his hand to his temple and reflects for a moment. "Let's see, let's see, was I eighteen? No! Nineteen, of course, I was nineteen! The teller of tales has to be exact.

"Then I was on the 'Good Luck' with Captain Contreras, and we were on course to Balzar." This time he strokes his chin and proceeds deliberately. "We would drink a little something during the voyage, but I was more nervous than drunk. This was because I was carrying on with a passenger who had promised me that we would go away together to see what we could make out of life. Where was she taking me? That was the problem. And she was a splendid female. What a body!

"The navigator, who had already realized everything, urged, 'Don't be stupid, young man. Why do you worry if the baby dove still doesn't possess the power of the sparrow hawk? Steady yourself, because the lookouts have already espied the seven staircases of Balzar.'

"As you know, Balzar is high up. From the barge there are seven steps to climb, one by one. I put on my clean rags and jumped, whistling to calm my nerves. We had agreed on a place, but she said that if they saw her jumping with me, people would talk ... well, good. I arrived at the place. No one!

"Each second I became more and more nervous, but in the end, I saw her approaching, even more provocatively than she had on board. She got closer and closer, but then she suddenly turned away without even looking at me. For a few seconds, I vacillated, disconcerted. But a woman who confuses you has you enchained—you'll understand when you're grown up. I resolved, well, to catch up with her, but as I walked faster, she got farther and farther away. 'Ah, bandit, you're not going to outwit me!' I said, and I started to run. The moon helped me to find her, in spite of my getting lost between the trees at times. There was a moment I was so close to her that I could hear her blood pulsing. Even now I can't explain to myself how she escaped. 'Hope that I never find you, Bandit!' I yelled at her to make myself feel better, and then I sat down to grumble.

"To be frank, at that moment what worried me more than the woman were the comments of my companions. They're going to pull my hair beautifully for this! I began, well, to invent a story to tell them, and right when I had it ready, I got up to return onboard. I hadn't walked far when I heard the murmur of voices. It's her with someone else, was the first thing that occurred to me. I moved toward the place where the voices were coming from, taking care not to make any noise. Suddenly, I discovered a poorly illuminated shack. A group of men were conversing on its stairs. When they saw me, I went forward and greeted them. 'Good evening', responded the eldest man. 'If you would like to come up, we're having a wake.'

"The night with its pale moon had turned into a funeral. A few meters from the small house, a white-haired man was sawing some boards, constructing the coffin.

"Now I had lost my prey. All right, I thought, at least I would have a swig and a chat, since there is always good conversation and a lot of liquor at a rustic wake. So I went up. In the center of the room was the cadaver surrounded by four candles. I approached it, partly out of respect, partly out of curiosity. And do you know what I saw, Raulito? What do you think I saw?"

My friend pauses with his arms open and an expression of revulsion on his face.

"What was it Agustin? What was it?" I have to insist because he is still paralyzed. "All right, let's hear it. Well, what did you see there?"

"She was there!"

I clench my eyes closed and, after verifying my astonishment, he explains himself. "Her, the one I had been pursuing, she was there, lying down, motionless! But she smiled. I swear that she smiled at me. And she was dead ... she had been dead for hours, since before I started the voyage!"

The broad kind face of my friend, Agustin, appears transformed by a grimace of terror. He was afraid. Without saying a word, he rises to leave.

But I can still hear his last words. "Since that time, I don't run around with women very much."

KID

"The day after tomorrow, Ninon will arrive."

"Ninon! Ninon, the...?"

He stops, truncating the phrase in the middle of his jubilant astonishment. Ninon. The greatest rumba dancer in the world is going to be there, in body and soul, within range of his eyes. Maybe he will be able to get close enough to her to perceive her breathing.

"Yes, brother, we must prepare."

"One must prepare." Chato repeats the words almost unconsciously. How has such interesting news escaped your small wandering eyes? But what is important is that Ninon is coming to him. Now this is not going to be just a cold celluloid figure, but a hot body in motion.

"Brother, I'll be seeing you."

He does not reply to his friend's farewell. He is still preoccupied with the good news. When he sees Ninon, he will inhale her smell; feel the vibrations of her body—even the heat of the blood in her veins.

Walking along the road aimlessly drifting, recalling the other rumba dancer he saw two months earlier. Celina had altered his senses. But Ninon, but Ninon...there hasn't been another female like her!

He pauses in front of a magazine stand. He will rent some and pay later.

"Read these, they've just arrived."

Reading is hard work, but contemplating the women who smile defiantly from the paper involves even more work. He will need more eyes to be able to simultaneously see so many splendors, to submerge himself in the rivers of firm thighs, and small volcano-shaped breasts with rose nipples. What would it be like to die in that vortex of paper? But Ninon is not paper. She has already arrived, and I will be with her. I have this paper, with fake women on it, until Ninon comes.

"Ninoooooon." He launches a shout as he rises to his feet.

His hot head and trembling hands show him the path. Only the blessing of grass will bring peace to his fantasy. He flings the magazine away. The customers' consternation and the proprietor's curses set him in motion.

The grass Ninon the joint only one Ninon paper women but no grass Ninon marijuana Ninon a little cigarette not even marijuana Ninon marijuana.

But where? At this hour he would not find anyone to lend him money. If he begs the store owner, maybe he would be moved to pity him.

"No, young man, you know that transaction is prohibited. It's not worth the penalty to risk the credit."

"Yes, I understand. I'm going to have silver."

"Go on, kid, it will be a pleasure to help you."

'Kid'. It had been a long time since he had been little. Now he does not like it when they called him that. He has not been a kid since the time his stepfather had initiated him: "Smoke it, kid, smoke it. It's marijuana. With this you don't need women or drink."

He was not sure about all that. The Mexican movies had introduced him to a turbid sensuality. But Ninon is an earthquake in his body, which brings him to tearing his own flesh with tweezers in search of the pleasures in his own flesh. Then he gave his tired body to a sex worker, and now he no longer desires the solitary bliss.

But Ninon…has been the key to his pleasure. Now he is going to be near her. How can he bear the terrible wait until the night of her fabulous debut comes?

Only the blessed grass can help him. He arrives at the corner where the young men usually gather.

"What's up, Brother? Give me a little puff."

They do not seem to hear him; they are so caught up in their task. They are smoking desperately, as if the extract from the marijuana is the essence of life. The one who finishes the joint, holds it between two match sticks, using them like tweezers, and then, when only a tiny piece of paper remains, he steps on it and curses it again and again.

"Why do you curse it like that?"

"So it will never fail me again, imbecile. You're a kid, you don't understand."

Because of his ignorance of the secret, the marijuana eludes him. And his friends belittle him by regarding him as a kid. They don't even give him a little puff. And every minute, Ninon is getting closer... Ninon...but Ninon...but Juana...

He receives affection from the old sex worker. He stays there for two nights, in the midst of a cloud of alcohol. Finally, he leaves with money in his pockets. He buys a newspaper and searches the movies page. There is Ninon, watching, laughing, reproaching him for his abandonment. Tonight will be the night, the night for the two of them. But until it arrives, he will wait with the blessed herb.

"Hey Little Boss, give me five small devils. Yes, now I have the wool...."

Now he needs a photo of Ninon, the paper Ninon for now. Until tonight.

He has already purchased the photograph. He lights the joint using the paper with Ninon on the cover. But during the day, there is always the danger of the police and the terrible **silence**. It will be best to go over to Juana's to dream with Ninon.

He awakens with a start at eight o'clock. He dresses quickly and immaculately in his best style, and leaves for the theater. He settles into a good seat in the gallery and begins to smoke his marijuana again. He smokes slowly. He does not want to alter himself before the time when his woman comes out. Finally she appears. She is the same as in the dream and on the paper, but now she is real, now in the flesh, now his. And with his distant eyes pinned like insects on the rumba dancer's hard thighs, he surrenders because now it is not Juana, because he does not love Juana, but Ninon, only Ninon. And he is hers, and he comes before her, convulsively, feverishly.

Ninon has gone, the lights are burning. But he does not see, he does not know. He continues abandoning himself to Ninon.

"Please, kick this one out. He's in a restricted area."

Shoving and kicking him, they carry him out into the **silence**.

"Miserable kid, get out!"

"Kid? No, no. I'm a man who loves his woman."

MEN DON'T LIE

My name is Pablo Granada; they call me Pablito. I am like any other boy, but I am not completely like the others.

I play, I study, I lie....Yes, I know very well that it is bad to lie, but sometimes it is impossible to stop. I ignore the causes. Oh no, I'm already lying. I know the causes, but they say to me, 'Are these the circumstances for that, or not?' Well ... they force me to? If not, let's consider my friends from school. Them as well? I think so or maybe not. Their lives are so clear and genuine.

Rene Garcia: nine years old, red-haired, with a black mole on his face. He studies little, although in exchange he reads a lot: adventures, Donald Duck stories, and comics. His father is a banker who frequently throws cocktail parties at his house. It's a pity, you know, the cocktails make Rene's mama sick. She has very delicate tonsils and can only have a little taste of them.

Lusito Intriago: the first in the class, quiet and pale. Why is he so sad? His classmates shun him. Since he is so busy, it does not seem like he cares, but I think it makes him even sadder.

Jorge Suarez: the happy living earthquake. He knows how to tell—or invent—some formidable jokes. All of us want him to tell a lot of them, and when he has to recite a lesson—an affair which does not interest us-- we form a chain, just like the ones the spies use when transmitting boring political speeches. Of course, you cannot hear very well, nor do you understand anything; but you do make noise and that's impressive. Finally, the teacher says, "That's enough; I will give you an average grade."

You believe that I have told the truth, don't you? Thank you! You are very kind. However, Mama lives to say, "Pablito, I have faith that you will stop lying when you are a man. Men don't lie."

Men don't lie. It must be boring to become a man—but maybe not, because men do things which seem like lies. How am I going to convince you that that is the truth from start to finish.

Two days ago, when I left for recess, I forgot a piece of bread in my bag. When I returned to search for it, I entered the classroom and heard a voice.

"It's a crime, a crime that I won't tolerate," it said.

Intrigued, I hide behind the door; they leave immediately—my teacher and the singing instructor. In order to find out about the crime, I follow them. The singing instructor appears to have something in her eye; every once in a while she lifts her handkerchief to her eye.

"To leave in the middle of the year on account of a trifle ... and why doesn't the father want to marry you?" my teacher insists. After a long pause, he resumes his needless repetition, "A crime, a real crime!"

The woman continues making motions with her handkerchief, but she does not say a word. I ask myself when the crime was committed.

Finally the Principal appears at the end of the corridor. Now, I thought, if they would only explain exactly what the true crime is.

"The instructor is going to practice the march for the parade on October ninth," my teacher reports.

The Principal nods and goes into his office. Once again, my teacher repeats, "A crime, a crime without a name!"

Yes, now if he is so brave, he will reveal what the crime is. But nothing: only the same story.

"You must think of the students, of the school's prestige. What are we going to say when you are at seven months and you can't hide the bulge?"

Now, you tell me: Wasn't the teacher lying by provoking me to such excitement with the revelation of "A crime, a real crime", and yet having it all come to nothing?

Men don't lie. Poor Mama! If only you knew that sometimes it is necessary to do so, not like my teacher did for pure pleasure, but out of genuine necessity in order to continue living...

Our school is tuition free, but since it is the best in the city, it is attended by magnificent children like Rene Garcia and Lusito Intriago, who live in houses like the ones in the movies—brilliant, refined, fragrant.

Since I live very far from the school, I can tell them that my house is like theirs—brilliant, refined, fragrant. That is to continue living...It is a spacious chalet with many windows. Everyone has their own bathroom. There is a refrigerator, a washing machine, a floor polisher. We have five maids, but the oldest is my favorite: she was the only one of the five who saw me being born. My mother's clothes are fine and elegant. She knows how to sing, laugh and do the most exquisite embroidery, but only for us; Papa does not allow her to do it for strangers.

On Sundays there are three or four guests at the table, and in homage to them, my Mama cooks. Marcela, a little maid as fragile as my kite, is delighted to help her. Every Sunday, they make me my favorite dessert—apple pie. Oh, and also some beautiful noodles which are long, thin, golden threads. How good they smell, how good!

After lunch, everyone goes to the quaint little ivory colored salon dedicated to music and reading. My brothers and sisters go out to play in the garden. In my room, I sleep or read my favorite stories.

As it grows towards evening, the breeze lashes the birds' nests in the trees and its murmur animates the green countryside. The guests leave. Mama and Papa go to the movies.

It is a beautiful dream. That is how I manage to forget the two narrow rooms which are my home, where all five of us brothers and sisters are piled one on top of the other, where Mama throws out her lungs washing and ironing so that we can eat once a day, where we fight over half a banana, where Pepito coughs all day and spits out blood from time to time, where....

But why continue? That's not my house. My house is the other one—the one in my dream. And that is my real house, the house that I love, the one I talk about to my school friends, because I believe in it, and ... so that I can continue living.

Only, now that I have told you about my house, I am left in tears. I do not know why....

A PRESENT FOR JACINTA

Her young hips have lost their happy sway, and her breasts and nipples—previously delicate and quivering—have become massive and heavy; so much so that her chest shelters her new, rapidly-growing rounded belly.

"That has to be from some brother...."

"Because, otherwise, her mother wouldn't keep ordering her to go to school."

"But now one cannot permit...."

The teachers gossip through small lips. It is necessary to inquire first and castigate later: the discipline, the order, the morality...and the urgency to know how it had happened.

Jacinta Chauca, previously a happy, young, dark-haired student, now surrenders her trembling self to the formidable teenager who delivers her to the interrogation one afternoon and goes away forever. She responds with a solemn voice, an ingenuous look and a valor which perhaps was given to her by the vibrations from her blooming child. "Did you send for me?"

Ten furious eyes bite into her insides. Jacinta contemplates them serenely, and her gentle gaze exasperates them.

"Have you realized your indecent state?"

"Given your audacity, what is it that you propose to do?"

"I...I. This...?"

"Don't you see that you are presenting a bad, a terrible, example?"

All of them talk at once, coming closer to put their hands on her.

Now Jacinta is afraid, and instinctively she moves her arms to cover her stomach, to protect the sleeping baby.

"I...This...isn't my fault."

"It was your brother, wasn't it?"

"I don't have any brothers."

"Then, who was it?"

"Tell the truth!"

"No lies, Jacinta."

She dries her freshly fallen tears and speaks.

It had been in Ibarra, five months ago, during the holidays. Her forehead wrinkles slightly as she weaves the story, while her hands wring the wet handkerchief restlessly. It was in December.

"On a silent night, a well-built man appeared. I was half asleep, but I believe it was the bus driver or the conductor. We went to Ipiales, because my papa is a dealer. My papa had left me with the rest of the passengers."

When she pauses, they rebuke her impatiently.

"And what else?"

"Continue, continue."

"He sat down far away; he seemed worried, sad, sad...When I looked at him, he was startled for a second, but when he saw that I was alone, he approached me. I saw his mouth and eyes were sad—so sad that they scared me. I thought, 'Has he come from a mental hospital?' When his face was close to mine, I wanted to scream, but he hit me and he gripped all of my small body in his hands. They were hot hands, a lunatic's hands, nervous hands. Was he crazy? I don't know. I don't know anything about him! After the thing passed, he went away as quickly as he had arrived. When my papa returned, I was afraid to tell him. Now the bus was full of passengers. I didn't say anything, I never said anything. No one knows it, only you."

The spinster's bosom rises and falls rapidly. And to me, never, nothing ever happens to me. In vain she had traversed the immense and deserted Liberty Beach at night. In vain she attended two or three masses every Sunday. In vain she had renounced lilac dresses. A man never bumps into me, not even a crazy one.

The large woman makes a gesture of repugnance. Look at her husband, drinking beer every day, and harassing the maids every day. And when they rejected him, his defeated lasciviousness threatened them with, 'You're doing this to me? Now I'm going to tell Gulnara to dismiss you and bring me someone better: a little rose who will be compliant...heh, heh, heh.'

The small young woman, who is accustomed to giving grand lectures about virginity, sighs deeply. Mine was more romantic and I have been lucky. After so much time, I have not become pregnant. Of course, I know how to take precautions...

The eyes of the teacher of Jacinta's class fill with tenderness, perhaps because this story resembles her own. An accidental encounter, a violent passion: it is the same. And we are left with a child. The minute passes, the child remains. She is the only one who continues dreaming, and she does not add to the chorus of indignant voices.

"We will talk to your father. It is a terrible case...."

"And a bad example, above all, a bad example...."

"The dishonor will be on us all."

The father, an elderly man with a timid voice, is not a smuggler as Jacinta had claimed. His hands are calloused from the daily labor of working the soil. When they question him, he tells them the truth: a vulgar story of two children who played a game prohibited by love.

The furor grows.

"Her corruption has made a mockery of us."

"She came to say that she had been raped."

"She never convinced me, the hypocrite."

"She always seemed like a good specimen to me."

With one version of the story or another, the single woman's pain remains the same. She had someone who desired her, who deceived her. I will continue going to mass alone.

"A violation is a social transgression. And it turned the girl into a kind of heroine. But this, this sniveling brat, surrendered like a female dog. What can a thirteen year-old kid know about love?" This is the large woman's judgment.

Then the single woman chose to drain a portion of her bile. "But you married at twelve, without knowing about love, Gulnarita?"

"Those were other times, Madame."

"Madame? Ma-dem-moi-selle!" the single woman retorts arrogantly as she moves away, and her small steps return her to her obsession. A teeny-bopper, but she has found her man. He probably has a firm chest, a narrow waist, and daring, powerful hands.

They accost Jacinta with their eyes; they follow her steps in order to watch the trajectory of her glances, always seeking out her curved belly, as if they want to penetrate it, to discover the strong and tiny thing which stirs inside.

The last afternoon she spends at school, they bring her before the governing board.

The director speaks solemnly to her. "Jacinta, if you don't have the respect for your teachers and your classmates, we want you to have it for your child, for whom you cannot provide a father."

"Or perhaps she has given it several," the hefty Gulnara says mutters.

The words of Jacinta's reply lose their color in her dry throat. But the image of her child, a strong and defiant boy, fills her mind.

"Don't worry about the baby," she says slowly. "I will learn how to take care of it. It's not important that it won't have a father. Perhaps it is best."

"Go away wretch!"

"Director, I cannot make a case for her. She is an insolent one."

"Whoever she is, this is the way it is."

"Go away, and don't come back here!"

As she leaves the school forever, the thin, gloomy, bitter spinster hurries up to her. She takes Jacinta's hand and deposits two bills in it.

"This is for your baby. Take very good care of it," she whispers.

LIFE AND MEMORIES

This morning, they walk further than they have done for many years. Now, worn out, they cannot walk as they had in days long ago, and he offers to help her. But he insists in such a way that she cannot deny him the long walk.

"Let's go, Mariana. I want to see the city. To see it, to touch it...."

She is a little old octogenarian. Nervous and extravagant, her dull lachrymose eyes peer out timidly. Her dark grey hair grows out disheveled over her wrinkled brow. Her clothes—the abandoned garments of a beggar-- stick to her sad flesh until they appear to form one object: a flower darkened by dirt and misery.

"But, Ramon, I can't lean on you anymore. And so many cars go along there...."

Scrawny and shapeless, her withered and terrified face shines; her small anxious eyes are almost vivacious. She brings along the pack of rags that she always carries when she accompanies her husband on their daily task of begging.

"That's not true! I still have the strength. And now I feel better. Come on, let's go."

They set out on their journey across the crowded streets. They do not limit themselves to the corner which, in recent years, has been the center of their operations. Walk, walk, and possess the metropolis. They are united as only simple people can be, whose only problem is to survive like two plants which have crossed their branches until they have common roots. They march out, holding hands and leaning on their old canes for support. Their mutual cooperation produces a single block of tenderness. They are so integrated, one into the other that they seem to have abdicated their own personal attributes.

A young woman looks at them with vague envy. She says to the man who accompanies her, "What wonderful little old people!"

"Huhumm." The athletic man examines them contemptuously. "But they can't even walk, they're wrecks," he says.

The woman does not listen to him. She continues looking at them sentimentally as if she wants to wrest the secret of their love from them. "Their love isn't in ruins," she rejoins, almost to herself. And suddenly she is walking along with rapid steps, leaving her athletic friend behind.

The elderly people continue their difficult trek. They have not unglued their lips since they left the house. When they arrive outside a church, he speaks, "Do you remember, Mariana, we christened our son here?"

"How am I not going to remember?" She moves her head in a gesture of ingenuous coquetry. "That day you were furious with me."

"Me, furious?"

"Of course, old man, you were furious with jealousy, jealousy."

"Me, jealous? With whom, you say?"

"Uh huhh, with all of the men. Your pride grew until your voice was worn out."

He stops abruptly. He looks at her mouth, at her eyes; then he lowers his head, guiltily. But he is also softened by the memory of those years when love was still a violent fruit.

"Have you forgiven me, Mariana?"

"Forgiven you for it! If I liked your jealousy...." Now she is also living those lost years. "How handsome you were when your jealousy was aroused."

They continue walking slowly through the sunny streets, so full of people and of memories which impetuously enter both of their hearts.

"Ramon, if we went where the godfather...."

Life and Memories

"What godfather?"

"The one who had the best records in the neighborhood—what was his name? Wait...."

They pause. She closes her eyes to dig deeply into the mountain of memories. "Domingo! Yes, the godfather, Domingo."

"Domingo?"

"Yes, man. Don't you remember how he would throw wonderful parties?"

"Yeah, yeah, but..." The walk has tired him a little. "Earlier you didn't want to go out, and now ..."

"Then, you don't want to humor me." She puckers her lips like a spoiled girl.

"Well, Mariana, if you wish..."

They gaze into each other's eyes and continue walking. Disoriented, she cannot find the right route. They are, well, a bit of a hazard, like old boats adrift in the middle of strong currents and cross winds. They know they are very far from their house; but they continue, he to humor her, and she because she is living only in her memories. His friend's house is like an incessant front, an interminable beach.

"Now we're close, Ramon."

"Yes, yes, we can't continue much further... We'll continue."

She smiles gratefully and drags him along more forcefully, searching for the lost way with her eyes and nose. Along with his tiredness, the sad memories arrive.

"Mariana, do you remember when I owed some silver to my godfather Encarna and I only paid him back part of it?"

She weakly denies it with a shake of her head.

"But don't you remember it was when I went out to buy the medicine for the boy, the night we felt so bad?"

Already their worlds of memories have diverged. She grimaces in annoyance.

"Now that so much time has passed, who can remember?"

"What a head you have woman, what a head!"

Now, each one of them talks to themselves, each in their own way.

"At your friend Domingo's last party, you hit this guy who kept pressuring me to dance."

"What did you say to my friend Encarna so that he let me stay in debt? And to his wife, who had a tongue more than anyone else?"

"But he didn't say anything to me about being in love. Which was much better than the case with the other chubby one, and you didn't even notice him."

"I wanted to pay him, but after settling the expenses for the boy's funeral...How handsome he was...."

"I felt good in that green dress you bought me for Easter."

This time, he says nothing. His legs are shaking and so he has to stop. "Mariana...Mariana...."

"What, little son, what!"

"I want to sit down, help me. And it's dark, everything is dark."

"Let's see, let's see. You are pale, Ramon, and trembling. Let's sit down here."

With difficulty, they huddle into a deserted doorway.

"It's nothing, don't be frightened. A little sleep...I'm exhausted." He yawns at length, half-closes his eyes and continues, "How sweet it is to sleep when there is no noise. We're going to sleep together, very close, like we did the night the boy died."

"Like the night you were infuriated with jealousy, and then we made up."

He has already fallen asleep; she can tell from the rhythm of his breathing. She covers his face with a handkerchief. "Poor thing, he has to sleep." She watches her dear old man, and says, "Today has turned out to be happy, very happy. For you too, wasn't it? We always were. With our son, and yet, when he died... it took away a lot, our illusions, our hopes. We were left so poor. A little while afterwards, we began to beg. But we were always together, very close." She rests her head on her bent legs and slowly goes to sleep.

Δ

"How long did you sleep next to your old man's corpse?"

Sitting in the middle of her tiny room, the little old woman wants to weave memories. It is useless, because the memories left when he did, and now everything is a nebula through which she transits alone.

"We were very close, then they separated us, and then...they carried Ramon away. And now, who will go out with me? And the old man is waiting for me."

She covers her legs with a few threadbare blankets and smiles coquettishly. "You're not going to be jealous when I join you Ramon; you're not going to be jealous."

She stretches out in her poor wretched bed, still smiling. In her solitude her old man's jealousy is her only memory. The rest have departed with his life.

A ROOM FOR RENT

White and deserted, the languid neighborhood displays its long narrow houses. Around here she does not have the ballerina ball to lift her out of her uneasiness.

Women and men, teenagers and the elderly alike, appeared to have definitely moved away from this particular neighborhood.

However, as the working day comes to an end, when the dying sun agonizingly sinks between the green heads, its rays entangled in their hair, its fingers curving towards an immense hand, it inundates the grey stones on the shabby paths with purple light.

A woman, more short than tall, pauses there, her constricted hips and bosom restless. She lifts her head towards the street, lifting the base of her small turned-up nose a little like a princess in an opera box. She observes the locked houses, whose worm-eaten windows hold one or more weather-beaten glass panes, where in the mornings the ardent silhouette of the proud winter sun would sharply outline her. These houses do not have plants or birds. Could the houses be deserted? Maybe they are occupied? No, she finally sees a gaunt, mangy dog begin to scratch a persistent flea in residence on its head.

She decides on a corner house. She knocks gently, almost without the wish to be heard, because the house frightens her. Naturally no one hears her. Recovering her confidence, she knocks again. Yes, now she wishes that they would hear her.

A voice muffled by the distance, jumps out from inside, and says, "Who is it?"

The door, which is densely covered with a fine layer of grey dust, opens. In the middle of the staircase stands the stooped figure which must belong to the female gender. The woman's severe eyes scrutinize her, furiously, interrogatively.

Without crossing the threshold, the young woman murmurs, as if she were dreaming out loud, "I would like to know if there are any rooms for rent in this house."

This one moves her lips without saying a word; she appears to deliberate. She walks around alone and wears very tight clothes; she looks like a good specimen. There are many in this neighborhood that...God save me from them.

At last she responds, "How many people are there in your family?"

With a smile playing on her lips, which are encouraged by hope and dry from fatigue, the young woman replies, "Just three, no more...."

"Are you married?"

"Yes."

"And, your husband?"

"My husband..." Everywhere it's the same, the same. "... is ..."

"Enough." The door slams on the dilated nostrils of her shy little nose, which she points towards the street. Bad luck.

She wanders through the streets searching for a sign, a door or a balcony that might smile benevolently on her, that might encourage her to continue her search. Three days without finding anything suitable, and I have to move. Move to where?

"I need the room," she says to the landlady who is grumpy and obnoxious.

"They can't live here. It's for women only...decent women. You? You're saying that to deceive me!"

"I'm sure it was you who said ...You said—" She pauses abruptly, and then says in a fury, "Is it because they have a right to demand it?" With a vague gesture, she pretends to smile, stretching her lips in a close approximation of bitterness.

She walks for several blocks. When she reaches a corner, a man approaches her.

"Between us precious, it will be exactly as you say it should be...."

"Stupid, who are you confusing me with?" She puts her hand out in front of the gallant man's face.

Flustered by the incident and believing that she is being watched, she enters the nearest house.

"Move on, move on. And don't worry about that one. He's a dirty man: first he begs, and then he demands a loan, for which the payback turns out to be eternal. I just put an end to it."

With a distracted expression, she talks to an exuberant lady. The high sleeves of her low-cut robe reveal the brilliant pale skin on her plump arms.

"We are waiting for you." She strokes her hair extensions and continues, "I would help you, but last night's excesses and, above all, the monthly inconvenience which we women endure...." She feigns a small cough and hits her chest.

"What are you saying to me? Who are you?" The disconcerted young woman manages to ask.

"How gracious you are! Perhaps you are not the one who we are waiting for..." She winks, then she confidentially insinuates, "... for a splendid client?"

"Me?" Aghast, she turns to run like a pursued goat. She runs until she has to stop. Her breathing is labored; her heart beats in her chest as if it is going to run her over. Besides she has to think. Evidently there was a misunderstanding with the man and the woman—they were waiting for me. What did I say? They were waiting for a ..., and I arrived! She extracts a handkerchief from her purse, wipes her feverish forehead and avidly, almost greedily, inhales the humid afternoon air. Somewhat composed, she notes: They aren't chasing me, no one has hurt me. Why run? She cleans the dust off her shoes, puts the handkerchief away and continues walking.

She enters a new small street. If only I could find a good room, without malicious porters or meddling neighbors...This street is quiet. Yes, the houses aren't bad, modest, without signs of misery. It will be cool in the hallways or in the kitchen bedrooms. I occasionally sleep late. Juan says it is healthy, and I tell him: 'Provided that one doesn't do it too often.'

A little further away, along the sidewalk, three children are laughing and jumping. As the woman approaches, they pretend they are about to leave, but....

"Hey, kids. Do you know if there's a place near here with rooms for rent?"

Calmly, the leader of the loiterers furrows his brow. In an instant he responds, "In that one over there. Hey, boys let's go show it to her."

They walk a few steps and pause in front of a dark doorway. At the bottom left there is a set of disjointed stairs, fetid from the dampness of an enormous gloomy house.

In a few seconds, she finds herself in a corridor with many small narrow doors. Which one should I knock on? There. It will be easy to ask, since the door is open. The curves of a woman are limned in the center of the room. Her hair swirls and quivers about her bronze skin, her mouth is bleeding through her fleshy lips, and her eyes are flashing.

"Ma'am...."

"What have you come for, Nosy? I have been beaten, so what? He always beats me. Everybody knows it. I'm married, I like love. And him? He's an ugly snowflake. That's why there's snow in the room, snow in his hands and even in my insides. Right? Now you get out."

"Ma'am, I...."

"You get out; understand?"

She moves toward the stairwell and inadvertently opens a door that she had not seen when she came up the stairs. In a chair covered with blankets, she sees a pair of rigid legs; dead legs, made of dead bone and dead muscle, that have forgotten the daily routine of walking. Instead they keep the woman in the hard chair. She peers above the thick gilt-edged crystal at the confused young woman.

"Who are you searching for?" she demands, making her large white teeth dance. They are the pure white that only dentures possess.

"I'm...searching? Oh, yes. I'm looking for a room to rent." Her eyes widen unnaturally at the crystal, which weighs down on the legs which had been....

"My legs used to be strong. They are now too weak to support this plump body. They must have grown tired of carrying it. How many more years must I put up with this?"

Suddenly she remembers the young woman. She raises her eyes to search for hers, and apologizes, "I'm sorry, Missus, or is it Miss?"

"Mrs., I'm divorced, but my husband comes to the house every night with the newspaper, you know?"

"We rented it this morning. You come back here after fifteen days, at the most. Possibly I will be able to offer you something. I have some tenants who I detest, because they cook with garlic...."

The words, 'They cook with garlic' come out of her hard and hostile mouth like acid.

The young woman nods her head. Slowly and sadly she descends the stairs which reek from the humidity of the enormous sad house.

FOR CHRISTMAS

It must be nice to adorn oneself in lace, colors and jewels like Mama does. If only my schoolmates did not laugh because she colors her hair, eyes and fingernails. What is bad about that? Certainly, my teacher paints herself a little too.

Ugh, it's best that Mama is not a teacher; she would start to grow ugly from talking so much, correcting homework and giving lessons. Of course, if Papa were alive, Mama would not have to work. Instead she would cook...her hands! Rosita's mama has tired hands with calluses.

In the yard behind the school Esmeralda dreams on top of the curly grass. She leans back with her arms forming a pillow underneath her head, thinking December, the month of joy and merriment, garlands and lights. Her mother promised her that, if the school elected her as the star—they would spend Christmas together.

"Esmeralda, I am looking for you."

"Yes."

"Your Mama has arrived; come. The count is about to begin."

In one leap, Esmeralda stands on her feet. "And has the sixth grade seen her yet? Of course, they laughed. Really?"

"No, no just imagine, they left because the candidate withdrew yesterday. If so, it's marvelous; one less candidate: a secure triumph. Marvelous."

After hearing this, she sighs happily, smiles at the grass, and sits up. "Well, I'll stay outside. Besides, there's a lot of noise. I'll go in later."

Frustrated, Rosita says, "Who can understand her? She prefers being alone. Crying or talking alone. Although she says she wants her mama very much, it makes her sad when she sees her at the school. I don't understand her."

Δ

While the teachers perform the final count, the mother confides in her daughter. She obsesses over the triumph. She wants to see her daughter in white, smiling divinely. She must dress her in the new shoes in honor of the merchant who paid with largesse. 'I will take you away for a walk, but before that, I will have a grand portrait made, in an equally grand frame: completely distinguished. I will hang it in the living room in the center of the wall, next to the diploma I obtained for good conduct way back in my infancy. The village and the school were left far behind. Only my diploma and my daughter will be 'The Star'...! My child who was sired by the adolescent with large tender imploring green eyes, who said to me one afternoon, 'Miss, I have a little money. You are a woman and you can save me. I want to be a man, help me.' I kept him for one week, but that wasn't enough to save him. Yet he left me with a daughter.'

Rosita: Esmeralda will be 'The Star' and I will be her first lady. Before, Mama didn't want her. Today, it's different, only I can't play or run. I feel tired and I always feel cold. They say it will pass soon enough, but it's not certain. I think I am going to die and I feel sorry for my new skates. Who will Mama give them to?

The harsh voice of an authoritative teacher jumps out from between her toothless gums. She announces, "The girl from the third grade...."

"Mine."

"I said th-ir-d."

"Ours!" Joy dances over the faces of a group of emotional girls.

At the same time, someone asks, "Can I buy more votes?"

"Ma'am!"

Sad and defeated, she launches herself out to the street. Her daughter would not be 'The Star of Christmas'. She would neither be dressed in white, nor would she have a portrait taken, and her own diploma would remain alone on the wall.

On seeing her, Esmeralda knew it was not her. Who was it, who? Who? She does not even ask. Why should she? What does it matter who it was? I no longer have a mama, and I will spend another lonely Christmas with those grimy mice peeping in on my solitude.

Outside the whistles, bugles and drums sound. And inside, the rats ruminate on her loneliness.

Δ

"Alba, take this small drink. The others deserted me. They went after the dollars...The very white man himself...bah!"

Without paying much attention to him, she counters, "I don't want it. You're already drunk."

"And you too, aren't you?"

"No!"

"How unusual, since it's dawn!"

"I don't see it as being unusual, but give it to me." She extends her fine nervous hand and empties the glass between her lips, which she quickly dries with the back of her free hand. She looks around. Not a good "chicken" in the tavern; just this foul-smelling, inebriated man. If it weren't for such "company", her money would be finished. This was the fourth one she had gone through that night, and he was nothing special. My god, nothing good!

"Let's go Alba, drink...."

"For my daughter."

"Because...she won...."

"Yes, she won." Alba sits up a little straighter in her chair and says, "I don't want drink anymore because I'm going."

"You said that ..."

"I did say that, but I'm going."

Possessed by a wave of tenderness, she smiles. She can cry, maybe even pray, but no, no. With determination, she approaches her friend to tell him, "Tomorrow I will be with you. This day is for my daughter—for Christmas, you know?"

FRIENDS

Can existence be monstrous in the eyes of those who know why they exist, how they were made, and how they could not have been created...--Charles Baudelaire

He has been looking for work for approximately two weeks and the responses are always the same:

"I'm sorry, I hired one yesterday."

"I don't want anyone now."

"Come back another day."

Nailed in a corner, the man devours the stewed corn. The unmistakable aroma of slightly hot, sliced green plantains fried with sausages fills his eyes and nostrils. The street is full of vendors who yell out, trying to sell their sun-faded merchandise. They offer to some, they sell to others.

The merchants' bustling increases, and the listless man hurries away to continue his search for work, or food…or at least someone who will give him a piece of bread…bread. Once he has it, he will chew it slowly, without rushing, gently, to make it last. It will stay between these rows of anxious grinders! It will endure when, he can barely feel it quickly slipping down his throat and transforming into a diminutive bolus, when it reaches his stomach—the vacuous sack, the empty cocktail-shaker that secretes rivers of juices.

Before that can happen, the idea of eating upsets his stomach, and the bread delays its arrival. Will it be much longer? No! He has to do something. He walks in a daze between the merchants, he walks until he is far away. He has to eat, to have something to eat. The idea pulsates in his head like a nervous tic, and the hunger in his empty stomach grows. It grows strong and vulgar like an ugly instinct.

He continues walking and, as he turns the corner, a large robust crowd appears before him in the street. Women and men, with dry faces and dark circles under their eyes, are walking slowly. Their black-cloaked bodies seem to drag the coffin along indifferently. From time to time, a sob rises up; a moan slips out, which is drowned out by vague murmurs from the men who cavil intermittently.

The penetrating odor of old flowers leaks from the midst of the multitude. A fine playful, happy rain begins to descend over the advancing procession.

He will not be hungry anymore; instead it is I ... Who says I have to be? Judging from the procession, he must be rich. And I'm hungry, very hungry, extremely hungry. He will be elegantly dressed as if for a party. Does he know this is his final party? Did he wish to die? No, no, no one loves death: life, yes, money as well. They are treasures for the body, or better still for the soul—mine—for my rebellious gypsy soul.

Δ

He arrives at the cemetery with the mourners. The wide door cannot accommodate both the entourage and the curious. The crowd disperses into groups which proceed docilely to the bier.

A weary, dense, grey silence rises, agitated and disturbed by the repeated echo of departing heels.

Suddenly, the sizeable cortege vanishes, and the corpse is left alone.

Δ

The boy is named Rafael. He does not have parents; he grows up alone the same as grass, or a cactus. Between jobs as a peanut seller and the distinguished profession of being unemployed, he assiduously patronizes a tavern whose owner looks after him. There he learns more than is necessary. But the young man dreams…

His dreams are fulfilled! An old customer from the abandoned tavern explains, "I am preparing a royal hit for next week. I need one more man. If you decide...you know where I live."

Friends

He walks absentmindedly through the south side of the city on the day it is supposed to begin. A few hours more and his hands will be holding money –lots of it, and willingly. Unexpectedly, a man approaches him. He cannot recall if he has seen him before, but the stranger smiles at him. He takes him by the arm and, without breaking his smile, asks, "Where do you work?"

Intrigued, Rafael opens his mouth without saying a word.

"Don't be alarmed young man. I'm a friend of your boss."

"Go on! You scared me; I thought you were an investigator."

Rafael protests, he wants to deny it, but it is useless. They lead him to the bloody body of his teacher and informer.

Several years in the reformatory change him... 'because they steal lives'....

They overpowered that enormous rubber tree, who was his teacher. So how can there be any hope for him. Especially since his humanity does not reach a meter and forty centimeters in height, and his girth is barely seventy centimeters wide.

I must work in one thing or another. In the meantime...The work must be enjoyable and have variety; if not, one runs the risk of being bored, always looking at the same faces and, on top of that, making this or that every day and week after week. No, instead I will constantly change jobs! That way I won't get tired of them, or the bosses.

After leaving the reformatory, he meets Celinda, a lightly freckled thirteen year-old with generous hips. She abandons him because they do not have anything to eat. Without a job, he cannot have Celinda.

Δ

He enters the cemetery. The clock has already struck midnight. An icy breeze blows between the vaults and, although he has drunk a lot of liquor, he feels a strange sensation. A moist stickiness begins to descend over his body.

Here in front of the mausoleum, he detects a murmur. Is it a waterfall? No, it sounds like the demented voice of a river.

The sky sends him weak rays of light from a traveling star. He must not waste time. He breaks up the wet concrete with a small crowbar. He also uses it to dislodge the screws by scraping at them. A pale, delicate youth stretches out along the length of the coffin. Fine, elegant clothes cling to his body delineating his long lean muscles.

With difficulty, Rafael's clumsy hands quickly wrench off the clothes. A little feeling of respect and exaggerated curiosity makes him shudder.

His skin is smooth and white. Rafael straightens. His kidneys are hurting from the effort.

Finally, he puts the clothes in a bag, looks at the youth and smiles.

"When you were alive, you kicked me and spat in my face. You were almost a child, you shouldn't have died. I'm going and…I'm taking your clothes. They'll do nothing for you, but for me, they'll bring something to eat.

"Good-bye. We are not going to see each other again, but now we will always be friends. Celinda, now we will have something to eat!"

SHOES AND DREAMS

Luis Arturo, tall, green eyed, restless and energetic, is the leader of a group of kids who study at the neighborhood school by jumping from a bush.

His home consists of two rooms: a kitchen and a communal bathroom—a decadent throne, shared with the neighbors, which is located at the far end of a patio from ancient history. Children, women and elders alike frequent the small cave.

Children, women and elders are permanently fighting to get inside. When Luis Arturo, the tenant's spoiled boy, the senior citizen's counselor, and the kid's advisor, decides to end the conflict, he arranges for the formation of lines and imposes time limits of three minutes per person and five minutes in the event of entering in pairs for those residents who needed to leave for work. Surely this cooperative operation is an enigma that can only be understood by the protagonists.

A similar thing happens concerning the washing stones, which are fought over after 5am. For these, the young man insists on two categories of turn: the first for the professional washers, the second for those who are only washing for themselves.

Luis Arturo is the first of five children who live with a short-tempered, domineering aunt, whom he adores and whose responsibility it is for the control and distribution of the turns for the stones. His father is a cobbler and his mother is an ass of burden in the miserable home.

People must live at home, but the rest of the world cannot be this cramped and dirty, overflowing with ugly crockery and unnecessary rags, stools, washcloths and plates scattered on four benches; which at night are transformed into uncomfortable beds like a gift from a bad fairy. In the detestable workshop those old, mud-stained, dusty, ruined, trashed, rejected shoes lie on top of everything.

Among the clientele, there is no lack of elegant adolescents who approach with a gentle breeze of the finest things; others resemble an ill-fated king on the way to the scaffold. They come for him to repair some slight rip, or to adjust a broken toe cap. Cocktail and reception shoes do not enter his father's clumsy hands, perhaps because they consider them to be without quality. They come to reassure our greedy stomachs, though they have little need for quality, that the customers will not stop filling the stew pot with food for Luis Arturo's family. If that were the case, they would have died of hunger, like Miss Engracia Guano, that svelte woman who vegetated in a very faraway place when she sat on the 'throne', and died at dawn on a rainy day. The medics said she was in pain, but most of the patio's residents affirmed that she died from hunger, since the spinster's pride did not allow her to accept alms from other poor people. Her friend, Luis Arturo, does not forgive himself for neglecting to visit her. With nostalgic eyes, he evokes her image: her vibrant figure resists the harshness of the years; her fine mouth smiles enigmatically; her expressive eyes illuminate the gestures of a broken woman.

A very valuable locket, a symbol of the ardent nights, is timidly exposed at her languid neck. On Saturdays at twilight, she covered herself with a fringed shawl from Manila. She was able to survive from the sale of her sparse furniture and knick-knacks. They found her three days after she died in an advanced state of putrefaction. She used to be so clean, and used more perfumes and cosmetics than her meager funds allowed. Her face's incredible freshness would capture the looks of the curious. The proceeds from the sale of the locket prevented the public collection that would have shamed and destroyed Engracia Guano. According to the expressed will of the deceased, which she had loyally written on a worthless piece of paper when she felt death was near, her bed—a rickety hammock—passed into Luis Arturo's hands.

Δ

When he departs for school, Luis Arturo lives in a jubilant world. He leaves the bad smells and the clotheslines full of laundry behind him. During vacations the women finish with the bathroom around ten o'clock. He expands his lungs to breathe in the clean, fresh, invigorating air. Far away from his tiny room, the pure blue transparent sky presents itself to him, and the idea of being an astronaut possesses him until he makes it his dream night and day.

He aspires to walk through the sky and laugh at the moon that used to be distant and a vain dream. He amuses himself by imagining how it would be to see the Earth from that height. Would it be a minuscule dark body? No! Somewhere he had read about a dazzling spectacle: the Earth splendidly outlined by its unshakeable snow-capped mountains and silver-plated seas, with the scorching sun possessing it! And if this plan does not work, he would go off to sea, navigating all of the oceans, searching for the origin of life.

He does not exclude the possibility that his dreams might fade away and that in time the skies and the seas would also fade away; he would resign himself to making things solely with his hands a tailor, a mechanic, a chauffeur, anything; but never a shoe cobbler! Poor old man reduced to a three. He evokes his father's silhouette, with his hands and his nostrils submerged in those dreadful shoes. Shoes, shoes, shoes! He approaches a mountain of dusty footwear, shoes of every color, every size, every odor. He selects a pair and examines them at length as if he were preparing himself for a dissection.

The owner of these must be a large good-natured person, who moves like a huge barge on the high seas. I'm sure he's lame. Well, not properly lame, just pigeon-toed. Part of his humanity rests on his right foot, on its outer edge. The opposite happens on his left.

He moves them a little further from his gaze and reads them like a book. *He has calluses, doesn't wear socks and has never been in a bathtub.*

With impassive eyes, he surveys the shoes which fill a good part of the two rooms. The workshop is partitioned by a brightly colored flowered canvas curtain, whose paint has disappeared in places from contact with his children's dirty hands as a result of their habit of spying on the customers. His eyes settle on a few sensational shoes.

Yes, these have the mark of personality. He fixes them with a contented happy look, sensing their smoothness is as soft as a glove without venturing to touch them. Their perfect finish dazzles him. *Who could they belong to? A minister! No! The President! No! I have observed it many times: chubby people can't be the owners of these feet, of that I am certain; these belong to a man who is tall and thin.* He delves further into the essence of the man's character; he glimpses a new aspect of their owner: a tidy distinguished man without calluses.

These feet receive a pedicure every fifteen days. They have a vehicle that drives them everywhere. They don't have to trot all over the city. They lay out in a bath for men only.

Farther away are some red sandals, a Bordeaux red, like the color of his friend Armando Lecaros' blood when he cut his little finger with a brand new American pocket knife, while boasting about being a great proprietor of a rare instrument.

These are a teenager's sandals: sandals without tiredness, sandals without sorrows.

He contracts his mouth into a bitter expression as he notices his clients are making a little progress. In twelve years, I have never encountered shoes like these in the shop. Now there are two pairs! Two pairs! And they are small ones, very small. He regretfully prepares to leave for his break. It does not bother him when he is stopped by a young man who holds out a bundle and advises him that he needs his footwear fixed that night.

He thinks I'm a mender as well; that's all I need. I could throw that bundle in his face. I check myself and nod as I maintain an aggressive expression on my face.

The customer leaves and Luis Arturo examines the shoes. His expert eyes capture the details in a quick glance.

Good leather, intact toes, ruined heels. This coward takes all of his difficulties out on his heels. He walks a lot, and has acidic urine; naturally he lacks a proper bathroom.

I think about father again... *Papa, Pa-pa...You never wash your hands before going to lunch. And those shoes. How can you lie down with them? Carrion, filth. No, I have to be ... Absurd! Who is going to pay for my education? And if my father stopped this, I would have to forget my dreams.* I look at the shoes as if for the last time. *This is not a workshop, but a garbage can, a cemetery, a sewer. And I slept next to him for seventeen years. I breathed that stench many years before I was born. Here they love my father. They love themselves; the misery unites them, and they bind him more each day. Here everything happens. Is that a home? No!*

Shoes and Dreams

It's a pigsty!

It moves away, leaving him perplexed by his father, who is just entering his workshop. *If I am not content, at least I've been a soldier with him through the years of his battle with his tools, his stools, his grease. At least I am grateful for this kingdom that provided for the upkeep of his wife, his children and his sister condemned to celibacy by her ugly loudness. He only anxiously desires that his clientele will not deteriorate: more ruined, tattered, older shoes. All of them would slowly march, with privation, but also with hope.*

One of his children will learn the trade: Shoe crafter! Manufacturer of handmade footwear! Creator of perfect models! It would be a shop that delivers luxury to everyone! A cobbler's shop for ladies and gentlemen! My God, what a store! It would have illuminated glass display cases, rock crystal mirrors, first class curtains. He would be content with keeping a vigilant watch over the workers. He would test them and demand a superior performance and a perfect finish. There is a great difference between handmade footwear and that which is mass produced without grace, beauty and style.

This is for his son, Miguel.

For Luis, the first born, the future is proving difficult due to his excessive love for books. Who the devil did he inherit that from? If I had the money, I would make him a lawyer, because the kid is intelligent, the first in his class, in sports. He knows how to give orders with a piercing look from his green eyes. The line and the list for the throne were his work – 'Three minutes for each person, and five minutes if you go in pairs.' If they spent longer, they would pay a fine. And when he believed the patio's residents would reject it, they all consented because they love him. 'Luis Arturo, there's a light cord that's not working.', 'The washer in the water faucet is damaged.' , 'The drain is clogged.' Luis Arturo here, Luis Arturo there... The boy never complains or ignores a request: 'I am one of you; you can always count on me.'

The third son will be a mechanic because he has the devil in his hands. Irma will be the magistrate. I do not need to worry about the last born; that one is still walking on all fours. He sits down on his stool, his companion throughout the years, and, as bent as the number three, pounds the leather sole harder and happier than ever. With his favorite song on his lips, he breaks through the annoying noise from the hammer.

Δ

The shoes move. He searches for his pulse, feels his forehead and finds no sign of a fever. Doubting his eyes, he rubs them energetically and, when interrupted by an unusual noise, resumes staring at the shoes. Now they rise up in a whirligig, whirling over Panchito and under Manongo, whirling like the one in the park, like in ...Without an explanation, the shoes suddenly stop as if they are following an order. Immediately they start to march, slowly at first. Squadrons of orphaned shoes without feet, without socks, shoes without legs, without owners! Luis Arturo does not miss a detail. He observes the way the older ones walk with short quick steps, trampling the younger ones which lag behind and are unable to avoid it. The shoes advance, surrounded by a violent dust. Black shoes walk, brown shoes take the lead, white shoes stumble, and shoes darkened by loose dirt surrender, blue shoes shake ferociously with clenched teeth! Sad undefeated heroes, they fight by continuing!

No one sees them. The young ones grow weary and they cause a scandal. They rebel! Surprised, the elders counterattack. Suddenly, some gigantic dark boots with an impeccable white cord rush in hitting with rage. The adolescents, the children and the elders unite in their defense, and the boots run. They run and run; they are not so strong. They go away terrified with their "giganticness", their shininess, their darkness and their impeccable cords.

Frantically united in their defense and triumph, they sing, jostling agreeably and, suddenly irascible, launch themselves against the elegant ones. The only two pairs in twelve years! The **unique** ones! Luis Arturo tries to help them and he cannot because something stops him; when he tries to scream, he discovers that desperation has destroyed his voice. He sees the magnificent shoes and the sandals without sorrow fall in horror.

To the ugly, dirty, old and torn comes the calm triumph over the solitary and beautiful, now defeated and destroyed. Now united with the injured, the journey resumes. With difficulty they move away, listening to a distant tenuous music, which gradually succeeds in reviving them. Led by their compasses, they advance smiling and dancing in his direction, for they love music without borders. The boy recognizes the owners by their shoes.

How well our basketball team captain dances! He immediately discovers that Herman, the best student in the entire school, does not have an ear for music. *He dances without rhythm or passion, yet he dances.*

The scene and the grey mood are illuminated by the unmistakable sparkle from each one of them. Now no one suffers, no one fights; the dance inundates them with love. Luis Arturo shakes and is transported. The music, his friends...He wants to follow them, but his legs do not obey him, because they are buried up to his waist, rooted like a young tree with new sap. It is not mud or Earth! It is...they are...shoes. Shoes full of evil holes, shoes with fierce glaring eyes. They are rising, they are smothering him. And how the damned things stink, how they stink! I hate you, carrion! You won't conquer me!

"Papa, Papaaa, Papaaaa!"

His smiling father caresses him. His clumsy tanned hands, so familiar with the carrion, are now warm, gentle and clean. No breeze could have caressed him more softly. Moved to tears, the boy kisses his father once, twice, ten times.

THE DREAMER

The siren is persistent, harsh and constant, like a dagger in his ear, or a cramp in his stomach. It eclipses all of the sirens, and even the memory of the sirens that announce the arrival of the New Year. Its rough moan pierces the morning serenade of the birds that, now terrified, rise up among the branches of a gigantic pine tree, their protector and accomplice in the escape from its lecture room.

After forty-five interminable minutes, it is a glorious dream! It is as if the persistent rain is a lover's whisper tenaciously penetrating his marble heart. The nocturnal concert of one hundred baritone crickets is a delightfully sonorous bugle. Happy and enthusiastic, the children swoop like blind arrows towards the school's sleeping patio. Luis Arturo is surrounded by a group that harasses him with 'whys' and 'whens'. The more forceful ones lead him to the friendly pine tree so that they can talk in peace.

"The program has two parts: in the first part is composed of The Ribbon Tournament, The Enchanted Pots and The All-You-Can-Eat Contest; then, in the second part, there is a fabulous dance."

"It's totally royal!"

"The length of the tournaments shouldn't be less than thirty minutes or more than forty-five minutes, not a second more. We'll ask the godmothers to record the winners' names and the dates, and also to give the winners a kiss."

"I object," Panchín says, "to my girlfriend kissing someone else."

"Stop the turkey business, a kiss is nothing important."

"For you!"

"This is not the moment to discuss foolishness."

"Is it foolish to prevent someone from necking with your girlfriend?"

"When a woman loves her boyfriend, kissing someone else is something like kissing a brother or a motherly gypsy, ipsy, dipsy."

"I oppose that and everything else!"

"That's enough, buddies!" Luis Arturo patiently interjects. "Panchín, would it disgust you if your girlfriend kissed them on the forehead?"

"Eeeh, ehh, that's good, yes, on the forehead! And I don't oppose it."

"That's the way to talk!"

"Secretary!" He shifts the attention to Luis Arturo. "Are the gluttons ready?"

"Of course!"

"What about the enchanted pots?"

"Yes, but I warn you, the freshmen from Course C have signed up. I think it'll be fair if we play them a good one this time in retaliation for the one they won last month."

"Clear, clearer, clearest! You clarify, you indicate, you walk away!"

"Silence, please. Go on!"

"You walk away; you point out; you clarify!"

"This will remain a secret between you and me." He looks at his friends. "If they enter in the middle of the first race, I'll know it right away."

"Clearer, clearest! You clarify, you lead!"

"Group secrets? I won't allow them!" Andrés declares indignantly.

"You leeead!"

"Secretary, I think our friends are right. It's best for you to speak for all of us."

"On one condition...."

"Set it free!"

"If the others learn about the plan ahead of time it will be because one of you has blown it to them, and in that case, they will already know what is waiting for them."

"We accept it since it's time for you to leave us; but soon we'll discuss it at length."

Intrigued by the plan, the group draws together into a tight circle. The secretary whispers his idea, thereby setting it in motion.

The steady, imperturbable siren erupts into the blue sky of a morning without history, pursuing the birds, intriguing the butterflies that precipitately take flight in fear for their lives.

The young men are also running, jumping, spinning, knocking, and crashing into each other like whirlpools on the high seas. After their euphoria they swiftly scatter along unknown paths.

How little those measly fifteen minutes of recess seem to last when there is so much to discuss, so many things to plan! Damnation!

Δ

A week later, in an atmosphere charged with huge banners of different colors and sizes flapping in the wind, the program takes place. Whistles, soaring rockets, and other strident noises confound and delight the residents of the patio. Candy and ice cream make the children's mouths water.

Young women and men exceed their most reckless behavior as they are excited by the intense rhythm and screech of the loud music, which has the virtue of transforming them into fresh, agile people.

At the back of the site, located in the middle of a street closed to vehicles, is a sign: Grand Glutton Competition. At its center sit eight chairs and two tables. These are occupied by the competitors, the secretary and a nurse—who is there just in case.

The competing athletes scrutinize each other from head to foot, gauging their opponents' stomach capacity. In their extreme nervousness, they cannot find a convenient position for their hands, which move like restless pendulums before hundreds of watchful greedy eyes.

One hundred, three hundred, a thousand pairs of covetous eyes encircle the overflowing table, caressing the food that is bathed in sunlight, intensifying its colors so that it looks desirable and appetizing. How, many wished they were participating!

The boys exchange greetings and sit down, closely observing the minutest details. The anxious eyes continuously survey the food which is so distant from their avid palates, their implacable mandibles—five bananas, ten hard boiled eggs, two bottles of Pepsi, and three loaves of sliced rye bread!

"Ready!"

It takes time. It's a sybaritic dream.

The most serene of the four, Pablo Diaz, gives the impression that he has found himself at a banquet. His companions do not imitate his expression, manners or attitude. The grotesque spectacle thrills the spectators who fully enjoy the speed of the contestants' desperate jawbones, and how the food seems to melt in their mouths. The smooth features of Pablo's freckled anemic face do not hide the satisfaction and eagerness he feels for the food and the prize.

Refined and elegant, Pablo savors the tender meat moistened by a **spotted** plantain; its sweetness is unequalled in the table full of food.

The Dreamer

Barely chewing and without savoring the food, his contenders fill their mouths—gorging and gorging themselves. They must win. They have to win. Eat and win. Eat to win the competition.

Pablo does not notice the whistle signaling the end of the competition. He enjoys his colas as they slide smoothly down his febrile throat, refreshing and also stimulating it.

It's fantastic: the action of the food reaching my stomach. My whole body vibrates. It revives me from a dream, I breathe better. If my brothers and sisters could see me, they would make so much fun of me!

He would live rejoicing, not exempt from a tiny melancholy. Nonetheless, he smiles at the gigantic hard boiled eggs, like those from a goose or a turkey; but more, much more appetizing, seductive and nutritious.

As he takes one of them, he notices the design on the tablecloth: a plastic one crammed with images of fruit and exotic flowers longing to jump into the celebration.

Mother, if you could see this marvelous tablecloth, mother…yes…

He puts the brakes on his thoughts; the presence of the hot loaves of bread, waiting and waiting for him, is torturing him. Time, a solitary shipwreck, escapes the uncontrollable waters from below. He has excellent manners. At his family's table, orphaned of sustenance, they had learned to dream of what they lacked. He always had that ability, that power. In the absence of food, and with a desperate vacuum in his stomach, he imagined he tasted stews and exquisite dishes as he was urged on by the infallible presence of his mother's silverware. Occasionally laughing, occasionally feeling the ecstasy of the marvels Pablo dreams about, she pleases him. Two of his brothers look at him with rage; Emeterio looks with sadness. *Well, I'll be damned, or the youngest brother will go to the crazy house for the leftovers.* His imagination scatters like frightened birds. He has it in his grip. He thinks he is eating small mouthfuls. He uses a napkin for the rose, green and red-colored juices he cannot swallow. While being content with boiled fava beans with salt, *zambo* stew or a simple fruit shake, he dreams of a banquet.

I ache for him, for his lost dreams, for my small brothers and sisters, for me, that we have never experienced good food on our table.

Pablo completely enjoys the banquet, without haste, without displaying his tender, sluggish stomach cavity that is accustomed to interminable waits. The pleasure of the regal banquet makes him feel bitter for the absence of his siblings who could not participate in the competition since the regulations prohibited it. And they did not even come to the competition since they were taking care of their mother. But he consoles himself: *at last they have made my dreams come true. It was worth the sorrow to dream and dream. Someday it will happen, someday....*

THE RIBBON TOURNAMENT

"Good God, today I have eaten…well!"

There is applause, whistles, teasing and Pablo Diaz endures all of it with serenity and stoicism.

"Today I have eaten, good God, the rest is not important because I have eaten well for the first time in sixteen years."

A group of The Exalted climbs on stage to remove him by force. Pablo, who is still dedicating himself to eating very ostentatiously without worrying about the public, the authorities, the contest, considers this to be sabotage.

Louis Arturo intervenes. He loves his friend and he knows his opponents are tough capable young men who do not approve of the impudent manners of the boy who can consume all of the food for the contest if they do not interrupt his impassive labor. The bellicose teenagers promise them a fight tomorrow and Pablo descends from the stage uninjured.

And now what am I going to tell my brothers?

Convinced of a magnificent comic note, the public applauds many times for Pablo and is unaware of the upcoming scuffle.

First they will ask, then they will demand to know the details.

Insistent audacious music envelopes the dusted covered atmosphere, intensifying odors in the blend of perfumes from the village drugstore and frying those up in a furtive bonfire that makes them vanish from the sight of the municipal **badge**.

When he mentions his participation, they will say, 'And why didn't you stop us so we could see your greedy pot belly?'

The fireworks continue their luminous ascent, cut back in their intent to approach the stars.

Pablo, tell us what you ate... Come on; tell us...Did they give you eggs? Plantain ...too...? And how do you know that? No, no, no we don't know, but we would have enjoyed it so much, that you might have eaten that....

A stream of laughter, music, and voices escapes from the open balconies packed with revelers like a church on Sunday. A few steps away from this improvised scene a bunch of children set off fireworks that finish entangled in a disagreeable smelling smoke studded with thousands of crazy sparklers that make the children run, the women scream, and the elderly laugh.

They will be sad, furious...I don't know. They will all talk like crazy cars in the amusement park.

From her sunless room Mama will say, 'Pablo, be good to your sisters and brother, make them a salt *colada*...I...I can't get up. Although this heat saves me a little on food, in the end...how it suffocates me and how lazy I have become!'

Δ

Several ribbons dance in the wind on a rope that barely stretches across the small street. Are they comets, capuchins, weather vanes? There are not two of them that are equal in size, quality, or decoration, yet the colors do repeat. At the far end a metallic ring juts out where the triumphant flag will pass.

"Pablito, you are making the *colada* without lard son. Ask our neighbor Lucita to give us a spoonful. I know you don't like to bother the neighbors, but we have to do it. Do you hear me? Tomorrow I will wash few dozen clothes and we won't have to beg anymore!"

Isela Ramos has instructions to kiss the winner on the forehead. The other super-civilized boyfriends do not see anything bad in their girlfriends' kissing the champion on the mouth.

Twelve cyclists race for the ribbon. Will it be yellow, green, sky blue, rose? Only they know, only they strive for them!

The crowd stands up, applauds, shouts, sneezes, coughs, chooses their favorite and holds the bar for him.

On seeing how pretty Isela is in the white scarf that emphasizes her queenly profile, Panchin decides to intervene. His jealousy tortures him and he intends to prevent the kiss.

The number thirteen is a fatal and arbitrary number. Panchin does not belong there; he knows it and so does everyone else. He is a very bad cyclist who does not pay attention to the jeers that the audience sends after him. He dreams of Isela's Love, Isela's Perfume, Isela's Flower, Isela's Song. They will marry immediately and go to live far away from the poverty, the suffering, and the pain. Why did it not occur to him to practice cycling? Well…yes it had occurred to him, but since he is so clumsy at sports….

The applause nurtures them with enthusiasm. Laughter and fears multiply. The jealousy confuses and dazes Panchin so that he cannot remember the color of the ribbon he adores. He searches his memory, he re-examines it once, twice, three times. It is useless, completely useless. He remembers one thing! Isela will not kiss him on his forehead or ear or hair or in the air, no.

When we marry, we will live alone where no one can see her or admire her. That's why I'm here: to love her, to take care of her, me and me, no one but me.

He pedals very fast; his jealousy and his dreams have disoriented him. He feels as if he lacks everything: light, air, serenity. He is suffocating as the evil applause drills into his ears again and again.

A fabulous triumphant shout of brings him out of his ruminations. The ribbons fly and flutter in the winners hands. Panchin is terrified….

Isela, who has won you? Tell me, tell me, tell me, right now because I am going to hang that trophy traitor!

The ribbons continue their gay dance, indifferent to Panchin's desperation. The bumps, falls, and zigzags confound him. As he scans the colors for the hundredth time, he notices there is only one. The wind rocks the ribbons vehemently, thousands of pairs of eyes are already on them as they rise and rise. But…then….

Yes, that one, that one...the citron colored one that we purchased from Doña Alcira Buenaño's Nenita Bazaar! I must rescue her; it's a question of honor: my girlfriend is not going to kiss anyone—the devil with the rules. Panchin races fast enough to see the girl of his dreams disappear with a strange, vulgar hand. I will not allow it! The ribbon, puff...but the kiss—I say no, never, never, never!

Curious, impertinent photographers contemplate the godmothers, envying the young men climbing onto the stage to claim what is theirs. There is applause, laughter, and kisses.

Irritated and upset, Panchin observes the victorious boyfriends and godmothers.

I have been an idiot. An idiot who still does not leave the limbo and those who are openly kissing their girlfriends a lot in front of the elderly and the crowd—that's the reward isn't it?

A sad princess reigns without a crown; a woman without love. Isela. Her ribbon is not given away due to a technical error by the winning cyclist and now her boyfriend is so fastidious with his absurd jealousy that always makes her feel ridiculous.

He is just like my Papa who examines Mama's shoes every day to check her journeys, who goes around smelling her underwear, monitoring her smiles and the words she speaks in her sleep, anxious to discover something. All of this is because Mama has a permanent brilliance in her eyes. Is such dreadfulness going to kill love?

She walks over to Panchin who is happily waiting for her since his dear little girl did not have to kiss anyone. And when she is beside him, he hears those hard, bitter, horrible words.

"We are no longer in love. Now we aren't anything, not even friends. Ciao."

THE ENCHANTED POTS

With the breakup of Isela and Panchín, the promise of the meeting between Luis Arturo and the leader of 'The Exalted', and the end of the banquet savored by Pablito, The Ribbon Tournament was finished.

At five thirty in the evening a violent drop in temperature is followed by an obstreperous rain with thunder and multicolored lightning. This forces them to transfer the pots to the living room, which is already decorated for the dance.

They hang from their mouths by strong knots tied with a thin piece of rope which crosses the living room from one end to the other. The tiny paintings, which decorate the bellies on the nine pots, attract the gazes of the children, who gather in front of a laughing clown who has a tiny button nose on a frowning infantile face.

In one of the paintings a thin, flitting parrot with a few feathers attempts to tell children horror stories. In another, an airplane with a broken wing and without a route loses itself in abandon. In one much further from that one, a fox sinks his eyes into a lively swallow that makes a show of flying in style.

Firecrackers, whistles, fireworks and torpedo rockets disturb the atmosphere of the pool room, which is The Exalted's hangout. It is rarely frequented by Luis Arturo since both groups detest each other. However, today everyone enjoys themselves.

A blindfold patiently languishes on the table at the control station. The leaders signal for order. The competitors smile stupidly at the crowd which is eager for an amusing spectacle.

Separated by about fifty centimeters, the pots display their round contours. Like festive hats, the covers hide their large mouths which are directly above their thick bellies.

Children, ten years old and not very tall, are asked to participate in the competition and, although they are ignorant of the pots' contents, everyone wants to trust their aim. Pablo Diaz is excited by a renewed enthusiasm. His siblings will be contestants in this entertaining game.

He obtains a spoon of lard with the help of his neighbor, Lucy; he prepares the *colada* with salt for his brothers and sisters; and he gives lemon verbena with pan sugar to his mother, who is sweltering in the burning heat. Then, freed from his chores and duties, he returns to the party.

They will try to break open one pot, two pots...Candies would not be bad prizes; nor would guinea pigs since, if they were not too beaten up, they would have descendants for a long time.

A bitter taste sticks in his parched throat. He scratches his head and spits angrily. He has not ruled out the possibility of being bathed in cold water or enduring prickly sawdust... no! The bad luck comes when he thinks about her.

Andres, the new tenant in the neighborhood, who relocated from Estero Largo for the Merchan family, was grieving because the pots, which were shining so beautifully at the party, would be destroyed by an anonymous, blindfolded, batter without scruples.

If Aunt Juana sees this ... she is easily irritated whenever things do not go well. I know her, I who put up with her continuously for fifteen years; but have not forgotten the wrangle she had with the political leader. He made a trifling mistake, and for that she made him swallow his dancing dentures. He was very beastly to treat her so badly, and Aunt had a good reason. I could not help her since I was a little louse who was wetting himself from fear. Today will be different!

Pots, casseroles, vessels, from the village, precinct, parish, are being slowly heated in the charcoal, rapidly in the firewood: pots that the city rejects. None of the ones from my Aunt are polished, nor are they glazed, but what good food comes out of them! The cocolón rice has such a flavor: I don't know if it is the earthenware or the lard from a corn-fed pig which produces the taste; with a lentil stew ... uhsshhuh. From it one knows the taste of glory.

Luis Arturo jumps when he sees the blindfolded boy aim for the cord. It is the first contestant and it happens that he is on the road to the gallows, this baseball player is driving him crazy! He follows him with his gaze, and notices that he does not hesitate. His head catches the noise which passes over him like drunken shadows. Next to the cord, two gigantic hands immobilize him and, taking him by the shoulders, spin him around like a blind hen. Convinced of the child's disorientation, the secretary gently pushes him. The boy is eager to strike a pot: Zasshh! He hits two, three, and frightens the wind which flees in surprise at his aggression!

The second boy's triumph is in spite of the sudden downpour the talkative parrot throws over him. The shouts travel through the living room, reverberating in a thousand echoes, and the applause breaks the blue atmosphere of an intense morning, bustling with shouts and noises. Doubled over by the cold, he kneels on the floor in order to collect the money which would amount to less than fifteen *sucres*. Shivering and quite content, he withdraws his left hand from his pocket where it was protecting the wet money which will allow them to buy so many things, while his right hand is busy wiping away the freezing water that flows slowly down his face and neck.

The child pokes at it, searching the air. He passes near, grazing one pot. Suddenly, the third boy's bat bumps a pot, strikes a pot, and a pot explodes. The flour that spouts out of the pot with the now split clown covers the boy's disheveled hair and his trembling mouth. He hastily cleans his hair and mouth. Flour, flour, flour for breakfast, flour in the corn boiled with salt for lunch...and those disgusting insolent laughs.

He removes the blindfold with one yank. Assured of his objective, he heads for his mother. No, it was not a question of...Was it a question of who were the devils?

Lucy, his neighbor, was right. First the absence of his father and, shortly afterwards, his mother's illness replaced work with a unique indefatigable cough. It began little by little. Its volume gradually grew and invaded the atmosphere of the humid room, stripped of things, overloaded with people and for a while, a little less lively since the flies and fleas would not give them a break.

"Wake up everyone," it orders.

The neighbors protest and murmur, demanding silence. As if the poor old woman could swallow that devilish cough—that whole commotion! The terror of death slides down her dilated throat! She looks at her children one by one with her anguished imploring eyes; so much torture! A compress of thin grass, a vapor rub and a big steaming cup of lemon verbena infusion prepared by her neighbor, Lucy, calms her; or we believe it calms that impertinent cough which has no schedule and no respite.

Pablo's triumph is not insignificant. In similar crowds, other boys would have garnered more. He was ignoring Emeterio, who was passing by him.

Pablo hates the mob that enjoys all sorts of nonsense. Without guessing what he is doing, he sits on a stone and stretches his tired legs...he considers his shoes: the right one is ripped and both the heels are ruined. The lack of shoe polish means they are always rustic and flaky. His discolored socks, with numerous holes, are a final present from the boy, Jacinto.

They shake in the environment of renewed guffaws. Emeterio feels the pressure of fingers on his right arm. They pull on it. The panting emotional crowd shouts. Whistles, fireworks, torpedoes, riot and riot. Seizing Emeterio's arm, Luis Arturo forces him to leave; but he resists, desiring to know what is happening. He searches for the source of the laughter in the gaps between the pennants. He collides with the puny body of his brother, Nicolas, who is running behind a white dove. Everything seems like a bad dream and they yell in his ear.

"Emeterio, it's the cough. Do you understand?" It imposes itself across the distance with its echo, its humidity, its impertinence.

Δ

Five kids hug, kiss and sink their heads into their mother's neck. Her cold face indifferently abandons itself to their caresses.

Pascualina gives precise instructions. The poor woman is so generous. She knows how to bring a child into the world, how to prevent a miscarriage or induce one, how to cure a bad eye; and, if she could have held a scalpel in her hands, she would have operated with confidence.

He sends the kids out and locks himself in with the corpse. Three quarters of an hour later, he again refuses entry to the curious by allowing the children in while deterring their friends and the neighbors. He snatches the death certificate out of Luis Arturo's hands. He examines the paper whose letters he would never decipher, and wrinkles his broad nose, which has an acute sense of smell.

"They killed her because of me. They cure the rich." In a voice without light she adds, "Someone must make a collection. She can't remain lying on the bed in mortal sin."

"Leave off the sins, Pascualina!"

She extracts a greasy envelope from her withered bosom, opens it carefully and extends a hundred *sucre* bill to him. "My comrade deserves more, but I can't leave myself without a *real*. There are those who guard the living as well."

"If you believed less in sins ... I am appointing a secretary right now. Mama Teo wants me to find one."

"Me, a secretary? That's heresy, a secretary, god wouldn't allow it!"

As Luis Arturo, leaves Pablo, the one from the banquet, intercepts him. Pascualina is waiting for him.

"I helped at your birth, son. Today you will help me by pursuing your new post."

The young man wants to reply, but Panchín stops him.

"This is for your mama. I've heard from mine that doves are good food for the lungs and maybe...."

The Enchanted Pots

FLORENCIA

Florencia's death produces complications for those who live on the patio. Some of the residents offer assistance or collaboration, while others only offer their cordial presence. She accepts everyone's assistance. She is limited by what each one is able to give: a rickety bench, two paper-covered stools from here; a pair of feeble chairs from she does not know where; free stock from the café, a gift from Mr. Anselmo. Two dozen donuts, a package of cookies and a jar of sugar magically appear. Doña Lucy presents her with an enormous pot from the cafe for boiling water. Sundry, chipped cups arrive in a well-worn basket.

In the hands of diligent volunteers three brooms carry out the sanitary work. The patio's hygiene is a complex and difficult task. The children as well as the elderly and even the adults have dropped bones and propelled papers, peel, and spit. Doña Lucy's protests contain every different shade. To mollify her, they organize a crew of workers who make the patio sparkle. Ants, rats, and flies are eliminated by the brooms and the D.D.T. She must think of everything.

"The neighbors, the coffin...."

"Have they already dressed the deceased?"

"We don't know because Pascualina...."

"Pascualina—what?"

"She won't let us. She said it's a sin to see a dead body outside of its coffin."

"That's true...and the old woman doesn't confess, nor does she go to mass."

"But if we have a full service for her—"

"That's not good enough! God is God and one must be under his grace!"

Isaura listens silently. As she fixes them with her electrifying gaze, a small caged shrew prepares to attack. She controls her ungraceful singer's chest and retorts with Olympic scorn, "If God is incapable of pardoning the ragged and those who are dying of hunger; if God ignores the injustice and the oppression, why do you serve a God who will never be with us since he is only one of them?"

"Neighbor, for God's sake!"

"Measure your words, Doña Isaura."

"Why?"

"Because there are true Catholics present."

"Catholics or stupid masochists?"

"I'm dying. What an ugly mouth!"

"Well die now, because that's the way things are!"

After the door slams, Isaura recalls her childhood on a windswept, dirty, remote beach full of mysterious rumors.

"Are you listening to me Florencia? I can't even see you. To do it according to what dimwitted Pascualina says would be a sin. The poor continue in ignorance. She was born that way and she will die that way. But I feel close to you, Florencia, perhaps because...Together we were invincible! We were as strong as the grass that rustled in the wind, washed by silence and soaked by the rain. Even though everyone tramples on it, it keeps its face to the sky. Like her, the grass sings, the grass dreams. We lived near the river, yearning to drink from its waters; the waters that caressed the bottom slowly in the hot summers and swiftly, very swiftly, in the hard winters. Its music was refreshing, its breath cheerful. We used to invent games and discover the nests of sad, weary, or sick birds. We caught fish that we would immediately cook on improvised barbeques. With our feet in the mysterious water and our sweaty bodies submerged in the sand, we ate happily. What banquets we had! We lacked everything, but we had our dreams and we wished for ... a miracle? No! The culmination of those dreams was two sons and one boat. You would go for a walk in that old river, which was crystalline and placid, patriarchal and wise, next to a captain with green eyes. Florencia, I believe those green eyes were damned....

"I never wanted children. My intuition was…perhaps…that I lacked ovaries. No, I don't know! I wanted to sing, and I sang—in the church choir, on the beach, beside the river and in the village festivals—all day and all night! There wasn't a time, a place or a situation where I would not want to sing. And I sang because I felt surrounded by music, by rhythm. I found music in the quotidian noises, such as a boy's weeping, a bird's flight, a boat's motor, the rooster's song, the sound of a crackling fire. I made myself a singer! Without any musical training, I promoted myself on an obscure radio station.

"Among gloomy radio announcers, tipsy guitarists and stingy advertisers, I left my girlish dreams and created a woman's life. They said: 'Isaura, tonight you sang and you were divine.', 'Isaura, who gave you your voice, your style, your perfumes?'

"The lark's song, the murmur of the gentle breeze: its persuasive words nearly convinced me.

"I never told her about the dirt at the radio station. She believed I was triumphant in a world where women were repressed by men! Her five squalid, raggedy children leveled her like a **wall**. It used to begin before the sun rose. She would go out with him, unable to find a set table or hot soup. On the verge of a nervous breakdown, she put on a wooden face for the shopkeeper at the corner store, who did not trust her very much.

"'What, at four *sucres* for the twelve big pieces, three for each sheet, and one fifty cent piece, a dozen clothes, rent, and food were not feasible. Hence, the staple dish appeared too frequency: *coladas* with salt, water, and flour. There was never the pleasure of a piece of roast beef with garlic and pimiento, or even a little rice with butter. That would have been too much to ask! Her husband grew tired of the odious responsibility of raising children who ate and demanded more and more. Finally, a boat takes away those eyes. Since they were not green, Florencia did not wish to love them.

"We learned about it too late. The absence of dreams hardens life, limits ideas, enumerates the hours, strangles the best thoughts and quenches the heart's fire. If someone had only been able to preserve her dreams, or to carry them ever forward like legs—what good disciples—and arms—splendid companions; and a nose that endures scorn and bad manners without moving away from the place.

"And now Pascualina objects to me seeing her because the dead woman is not in her coffin. Pascualina, the stupid girl who was raped at age twelve by her patron and teacher, and who left the university after the third year in order to practice the profession in the secure knowledge that, in the land of the blind, the one-eyed man is king!"

She consults her watch. She has time to do her radio program at six. She will come back to pay her respects to the dead. She will not attend the wake; she detests the absurd gaiety surrounding the dead, and despises those lewd men and winsome women eager to have a good time at any opportunity.

She tidies herself a little in front of a small mirror. Opening her purse, she discovers that she does not have a handkerchief. As she quickly rummages in a drawer of her vanity table, the appearance of a forgotten portrait gives her a shock and makes her sit down. With ecstatic eyes, she contemplates the image of a young smiling woman. On the reverse are the words: For the love of my life, Isaura.

"There were other times sweetheart, how much we loved you! And, though you ran off with that one, he did not even have the green eyes you longed for. My kisses weren't important to you, nor were the songs I learned for you. You traded it all in for a virile chest: ah, women, women, women, always running after the men!"

THE COFFIN

The simplest of coffins is inaccessible to the children responsible for burying Florencia.

The collections, which began on the patio and extended to every neighborhood, have raised three hundred and fifty *sucres*. The cheapest coffins at the mortuary are not less than six hundred and fifty. In their endless search, Pablo and Luis Arturo, traverse the city from one end to the other. They find coffins with soft cushions covered with the best satins and decorated with rococo borders; and ones with the finest veneers and luxurious handles that give the spacious caskets a light touch of magnificence. They can find better ones; it is all a question of money—**the wool, the twine, that stuff**.

"Even until you are in the grave, you can be elegant when you have it."

"And why do you need it if can't enjoy it anymore?"

"It's the triviality that I hate, you know? It's like pubic hair."

"Or do you want to be like them?"

"No, I only want to be a man, to be human. And more money helps with that because it gives you respect, prestige."

"Silly talk!"

"Poverty, I could like, but not misery! Not misery, because you lose your dignity, you accept scraps, you get used to begging, and you turn into a bum. Do you see the difference?"

"Of course! The worst of it is that everything isn't shaking and moving forward."

"I agree! What can we do without enough money?"

"It occurs to me that we could go to see Mr. Mateo."

"Give me the... mate who...passes water?"

"That's the one! He lives behind the mangrove swamp. He builds houses, beds, boxes."

"And if we buy it from him for six hundred and fifty, paying only the first half—"

"Pfff, not in your dreams: that's impossible. We don't have a guarantee and that's the first thing he'll ask us for."

"Sure, Brother!"

Δ

A rotten tree. Mr. Mateo possesses a grave countenance. His small deep-set eyes peer out with distrust. At times they give one the impression that the air and the light hurt them. It seems as though he is not listening when you talk to him since his gaze is looking behind you for something that only he can see. His dirty clothes stick to him, and make him look like a gigantic skeleton that stoops when he walks and is dragged by the wind. Large, wrinkled but still vigorous, his long-fingered hands, spotted with paint, move with agility and nervousness. The rest of his body lacks vitality.

The young men talk. Mr. Mateo barely hears them. They were surprised on the stairs to his rustic shack which is raised over a marsh and hidden by a dense mangrove swamp. Their gaze follows a leaden cloud which glides by morosely.

The old man's attitude leaves them astonished and they exchange looks, making plans for their immediate get away.

"This **man** is crazy!"

"He seems like a senile idiot!"

Trembling with fear, Pablo tries to pull his companion away and leave precipitously.

"Wait, wait a little longer; I'll be finished soon."

Paralyzed by that voice, they gaze at each other. Slowly they turn their heads to search for his eyes, to locate the old man's voice. His eyes observe the young men's feet. He notices that they are ashamed of their worn-out footwear which they rub one against the other without achieving the goal of cleaning them. The old man ignores the presence of the feet in the soiled shoes. His eyes have penetrated through the various layers of mud that hold them together. This new attitude disturbs them even more. Mr. Mateo is excited!

"Mine will be a grand death, then I will enter the ground in order to leave my dirty worm-eaten exterior and transform into a tiny song bird; and, without coldness, I will surprise Nicole! Nicole is waiting for me, yes. I know it." With a strange enthusiasm and with his eyes fixed on the sky, he talks and talks. "I know it because that cloud converses with me. It tells me everything: if Nicole is sad, then it goes away with the breeze; if she doesn't want to play or if—"

"Mr. Mateo, we—"

"I already have the coffin! I've made preparations for the funeral and the guests! Follow me!"

With his serious face inflamed, his skeletal structure acquires the agility of an adolescent. They climb the stairs to the carpentry workshop, so full of work tables and tools in absolute disorder that one can barely walk. Guided by Mr. Mateo, they enter a second room dominated by a deep penumbra. At the center of the room, a red casket sits on top of stools. Inside it are hats, pennants, banners, six pairs of white gloves and an abundance of paper flowers. In the corner of the room are two dozen spermatozoa of different colors covered with dust.

The boys are shocked. It is impossible not to doubt Mr. Mateo's sanity. They will have to leave at a run. Radiant and irrepressible, the old man, whose eyes and nostrils are now dilated, is jubilantly searching for something which he finally finds—a yellowed notebook, full of circles and horizontal lines drawn in pencil.

"Here are all of my friends who...!"

"Friends?"

"...are waiting for me so we can travel together. See, see, their signs, their names and their—"

"Mr. Mateo, we came—"

"...for a coffin. I have searched everywhere for a coffin, a coffin, a coffin! She was beautiful. A coffin, a coffin, a coffin! I will prepare things immediately. I need a woman, one more woman for my funerals. I have rejected all of the ugly ones. I refused, that's why I don't have the necessary number. The women and the flowers will go in front, behind them the bass horns, grieving for me from the lips of angels! The children and the banners will follow my casket, that great big red coffin you have just seen. The horns are the best part of it! Have you heard of horns being buried with the dead?"

"No!"

"The horns play the glory, the horns start the battle, the—!"

"Sometimes—"

"Never! A profound lament will accompany my body. Little by little my soul will separate from the rough bark that confines it and, look over there...through that window; my soul is searching for Nicole ... Nicole, Nicole...."

"Who is Nicole?"

"Don't you stupid boys know? Has there ever been such ignorance? Nicole is the air, the sun, the water, the aroma, the love! She's waiting for me behind that cloud which is white; like the cloud, she is white, white. And she is beautiful like the cloud."

"It's useless. It's best for us to go!"

"It's not useless, because she is waiting for me! Here are my hands, living for her, and my voice, which I guard avariciously, jealously for her."

"Let's go!"

"Yes, let's go boys to make the last coffin!"

THE WAKE

At seven o'clock in the evening, three bottles of *aguardiente de caña* arrive. Toribio, the neighborhood butcher, believes in god and in Golfin at wakes. His clever hands shuffle the deck of cards with dexterity and a keen balance, while skillfully holding four or five ounces of a shot of *aguardiente de caña*. The men hum and hum, sharpening their long white-bladed knives. The metallic sound, together with the taste of recently killed and butchered meat excites them; but it frightens the women and children who are convinced of their extravagance.

New guests arrive soon after the bottles of *aguardiente de caña*. Around ten o'clock, when the alcohol begins to eat into the meat, Toribio organizes a game of Golfin, which eclipses the gossips' lamentations. He refrains from the prayers and furtive speeches being held beside the corpse.

Women and men are given the names of fish that inhabit the Daule River, which is swollen in the winter and narrow and sparse during the summer: Dica, Corvina, Boccachico, Lisa, Robalo, Vieja, Guanchiche, Dama, Pez-Espada, Raspabalsa, Carita.

The first one on the right automatically becomes the compere.

"Golfin, Golfin the good whale, who is spoiled?"

The second man on the left answers loudly, "Dica is spoiled!"

"Dica isn't spoiled."

"Then who is?"

"Guanchiche!"

"Not Guanchiche either!"

"Yes, yes, Carita is spoiled!"

"Naw, Carita ain't spoiled!"

"Pez-Espada! Pez-Espada!"

"Catch him, catch him! Pay right now!"

A watch, a ring, cash, sunglasses and wallets are deposited in a ballot box. The announcer holds the key. The penalties increase or decrease in amount according to the quantity of alcohol consumed, the confidence of the accusation made by the announcer, or his relationship to the accused. When he has collected many pledges, he proceeds to deliver the sentences.

"Attention, ladies and gentlemen, attention! Pez-Espada, stand up, go out onto the patio and shout, 'My wife threw me out for…peeing continually!' three times."

"Not that!"

"Yes that. Yes! Yes!"

Laughter, jokes, witticisms, open flirting. The sentences turn spicy, beginning to degenerate to those which might end with the arrival of the police.

"Golfin! Golfin the good whale, who is spoiled?"

"Lisa is spoiled!"

"Lisa isn't spoiled! Bagre is spoiled!"

"Not Bagre! Bagre isn't spoiled; spoil Dama!"

"Dama, Dama …"

"Dama and Bagre wait to hear your sentences."

"If it's intended for us, don't wait any longer."

"Now then, release her Bocachico!"

"I released her. I want Dama and Bagre to go out onto the patio and … firstly, as if by magic, imagine Dama's whole body is turned into a mirror. Secondly, Mr. Bagre looks into the mirror and observes how an itch progresses on the front lower part of his torso; he scratches, he scratches harder."

"Three rah's for the Golfin's penalties! Rah, rah, rah, for the penalties!"

"I protest, you prick! That's not how it's played; not like that!"

A man with sinister eyes and a somber expression leaps from one corner of the room. He suddenly pulls Dama, who has turned into a mirror and is mimicking Bagre's obscene gestures, out of the way; and knocks Bagre down with two punches. Bagre's head strikes the cement floor with a dull sound. The man's violence silences the laughter, and the guests hold their breath.

"Jesus, Ave Maria!"

"Who conceived without sin," some elderly women outside of the game respond in a chorus.

On the ground, the unconscious man snores. Two shaken women kneel down beside the fallen man. Toribio Villao helps the two women. Meanwhile the man continues pushing and shoving Dama after she has stopped being a mirror.

"They are heretics and profaners of the peace of the dead."

"Heretics or not, they confuse wakes with taverns, beautiful god."

"The game isn't bad; it's what happens after the drunkenness which makes it go too far."

"It's midnight! Let us pray!"

With a powerful scream from the bottom of his throat for god to save him, Emeterio enters. "Pascualina, 'The Exalted' have two of ours!"

"I'm going to get them, dammit! God and our deceased forgive us!"

The Wake

It is barely midnight and the thirsty guests have finished the bottles of liquor. Some pale, greenish women drink coffee with donuts. Next to Florencia, two of her children snore placidly. The deceased lies in peace, but the peace is interrupted by the arrival of a woman.

"Bagre is dying in the hospital! Oh my god, Bagre is dying; we must search for that man!"

"The one that we saw kill Bagre?"

"So, can it be that Bagre is dying on us?"

"That's what they say, pal."

"I'm going to shuffle. What a pity."

"And he's so poor that his wife can't even offer us a bad Golfin."

THE EXALTED

He delivers the death certificate to Pascualina, withdraws from the wake, postpones the preparations for the dance, and leaves for the meeting. He decides to take a run on his luck; Pablo Diaz does not abandon him.

He sees them waiting for him in an old deserted alley, next to the fenced lot, which is the site for the upcoming fray. He also realizes this abandoned alley ends in an abyss, and he cannot elude the cold sensation that runs through his brain. They feel a pit in their stomachs; their minds are blocked. They have fallen! No one will come to help them! They are in their hands.

The leader of 'The Exalted' is the first to speak. "I wouldn't expect less from you."

"Well, I'm here for whatever you want."

"Well, well, if it isn't the little macho boss for the neighborhood group of thinkers: advisor, guide, tutor and executor for the residents of the patio, and ... future son-in-law of the never well-loved Mama Teo."

"I am Macho man, or human being, if you prefer; not a little macho, not a bully, not a troublemaker. You can say what you want."

"No, no, I'm not going **to say** anything; but, yes, I'm going **to decide**. Why do you think I made you come, genteel son-in-law?"

"Unmh ... I don't know." Luis Arturo projects an air of calm that he is far from feeling.

"Don't hurry yourself ... you will know! Hey guys, come over here."

One by one, they come in a single file line: several long, brown, solid bow-shaped legs carry him by force to face his stupefied companion, who is immobilized by two arms pointing narrow switchblades at him.

Their limber muscles hold him in mid-air as they pinch and sink their fingers into him. For a few instants, he straightens his head, which wobbles like a destroyed idol, while his body takes grotesque positions from the impetus of their jostling muscles.

Luis Arturo attempts to defend himself and to shout. He changes his mind when a chorus of raucous obscenities eclipses his voice with its shadow.

Ipso facto, they had tied Pablo to a tree trunk and blindfolded him with a handkerchief that had been soaked in foul smelling putrid water. His friend's screams alarm him because now he cannot even see him. His fears increase when he stops hearing them altogether. The sound of stifled breathing rises from among the vicious laughter. That is not just someone's breathing! Is it a bellow? Is it the roar of an injured beast or...are they raping him?

Although he feels physically weak, he still has a moral integrity which prevents him from crying, because he does not want anything else.

Ten minutes pass—ten minutes with the taste of eternity. The weary lissome arms drop the body on the damp grass at the far end of the large playing field, beside the unpaved road.

"Great!"

"Now for the other one!"

He is terrified for his friend, who is maybe dead, maybe abused, and he listens...listens for his own turn. He cannot control his bladder, so it bursts, soaking part of his pants leg. It causes amusement in the group as they prepare to attack.

Without removing the blindfold, they drag him from the tree and devote themselves to harassing him, by forming a circle around him, and striking him with branches previously dipped in warm tar. These sting.

"Here's the new Jesus!"

"No, he's the messiah!"

"No, no this is the bad thief, because he finished all of the food at the contest!"

Their bursts of roaring laughter sound like tin cans and attract two children who are on their way to the playing field in search of objects that furtive lovers may have lost in the darkness. On observing the scene out of the corner of their eyes, they leave frightened.

Relishing what they believe to be their triumph over the good-for-nothings from the patio, Jacinto orders them to put the boys in a line with their arms and legs tied to their bodies. Luis Arturo has to gain time while they are distracted!

With feminine grace and the coquetry of a stripper, he removes his pants to reveal a red bikini bottom with blue diamonds. And then waving it, waving it, he slides sinuously over the first boy. At head height, he kneels, absorbed and somber as if it were a strange rite, made to coincide with him forcing his cold penis into the boy's mouth. He stands up: graceful, lean and agile. He signals to his friends with the slightest movement of his head, and still waving the red bikini bottom with blue diamonds, he moves away swaying. Hoarse from shouting and laughing, hysterical and in tears, they applaud Jacinto and quickly imitate him. Before they have all had a turn, tremendous shrieks invade the playing field. The panic spreads! Pascualina arrives, armed with a garrote and several volunteers.

Without feminine grace, with his pants in his hands and necessary speed, Jacinto leaves at a run with his friends close behind him. They are leaving; all of them are following Jacinto.

Pascualina attends to the two injured boys whose testicles have grown enormous. She unties her friends and they leave in the direction of the patio.

DOÑA LUCY

It is impossible for them to meet at the burial, due to their appalling appearance and because they are devastated by a wretched state of emotion. Not wanting to be seen by the neighbors, they go to Engracia Guano's old room, which has been converted into an office with the permission of Mama Teo. She wants a husband for her daughter who is filled with respect for the morose tenants. Who would be better than Luis Arturo who is coveted by many decent young women? No one deserves him more than the heiress of the patio, who has jewels, sheep, and land with borders so vast that one cannot remember where their boundaries are. Mariano Macas was convinced that he would obtain the best husband for his daughter; unfortunately he departed before he anticipated.

Ah, your gouty legs, once they were massive and roving—always virtuous because they only opened for your Mariano. If they hadn't kept you in bed for weeks, you could have devoted yourself to methods for finding someone capable of improving the sheep's dung blood of your in-laws. We nip at your sex, but they humiliate us and we make them cry too.

In the small office, they resolve the problems, complaints, and conflicts of the patio. Mama Teo is insistent about marrying off her daughter; and, for lack of a better candidate, she relies on Luis Arturo to be her inevitable future son-in-law. *The son of a lowly cobbler, my God!*

"Our revenge will be more than perfect. We will prepare for it very well, and it will make history."

The teenagers stop because the patio is silent, even though it is five o'clock in the evening. The closed doors do not creak; not even an obstinate fly passes by for them to hear. The rats, assiduous visitors who fight with the children over pieces of tripe that they use to amuse and distract their stomachs for hours, until the possibility—it was not a certainty—of lunch's arrival, seem to have changed *barrios*. The washing stones, which are a source of great contention, languish, waiting for the cleaner's arthritic hands. With those hands, the stones do not feel lonely, nor can they live without having fresh water shaken over them. It softens them and makes them tremble; nevertheless, they still know how to caress their bellies, and this makes the cold water dance every day at dawn.

The cluttered kitchens, devoid of fire, only breathe with abandon after they perceive noise from the throne. However, the timorous are certain it is Engracia Guano looking for Luis Arturo.

After laughing, they cry and cry. If Pascualina had not arrived, we would be dead.

Neither the shaking nor yanking, nor the pricks and pinches, had injured the young men as much as the display of their genitals. I never suspected that 'The Exalted', at the height of their euphoria, would be such a mouthful; and they did not turn into murderers thanks to the firm presence of Pascualina, together with a group of volunteers.

It reaffirms Doña Lucy's theory, with the qualification that absolutely all of the tenants are **salted**. The past twenty-four hours had produced: Florencia's death, the despairing agony of Luciano, and the Golfin player who was carried into the hospital by three elderly women—the men did not want to compromise themselves with the law. Of course his friends are outraged. Since then, a growing number of neighbors have resolved to clean their rooms with a **red glove** in order to drive away the bad luck. They will make something in the cherry garden where Florencia used to live. Doña Lucy's hot hand does not go there frequently. She possesses the largest bosom, which could have nourished a few hundred generations; however, her maternal dreams were frustrated by her husband who forced her to have her ovaries removed.

He does not want to overload her with work, or to share her. He requires the presence of love in his life without flattery. He never suspects that perhaps the lack of children would unleash a profound fury in him towards all things uterine. Nobody on the patio ignores it; no one dares to comment on it. The good fairy is protecting them, which includes helping some confused teenagers. No, it is not perverted, nor seductive, nor infantile, and it never gives its initiates a second opportunity.

Smiles, caramels, and cookies are distributed on Saturday nights when she organizes an open-air cinema. The television and radio are her property; yet leaving them at the disposition of the patio makes it beneficial for them to aid her in her profitable adulteries. They despise her husband who forced her to dig until she gave him the twenty-two carat gold tooth, together with a digested chunk of fritter, and then left her as if she were a widow. Poking with patience and skill, she extracted the eagerly awaited trophy from a mustard-colored dreg that was sour and slowly thickening. That very day, when her husband goes to a soccer game, she savors a visit from her new love who is a clerk at a commissary—with fruit, eggs, birds from the coop, and money! Real money—they do not accept checks. And they enter through the front door!

"Pascualina will tell us how they were injured and we will search for the others and punish them."

At around five-thirty in the evening, Florencia's companions return from the cemetery. The friends descend on Engracia Guano's room ready to make plans for the loss.

She skips the funeral festivities and serves sandwiches and a pitcher of lemonade with lots of ice. For the tortured ones, there is hot tea with small fresh meat pies, soap made from cow's bile, and a liniment for rubbing and massaging their muscles.

"This woman is worth her weight in pure gold."

"Puaff, I detest adulterers!"

"Even with that son of a whore for a husband?"

"It's not right, because in spite of all that, he loves her; he works hard for her!"

"It would be nice if that pig wouldn't do that."

"My friend, I believe you have fallen in love with that high voltage machine."

"And if that's the case…what of it?"

"Nothing! You are only wasting your time. She did it the first time all by herself! She has never repeated it, and she does not have eyes for men from the patio. She is the best sexology manual in the country."

"Good, we'll leave that to Doña Lucy and her liaisons—first things first."

After two hours, the perfect plan is ready. They will teach them a lesson. Pablo suggests that they be on the lookout for the secretary from the commissary. Luis Arturo does not agree. Only cowards seek protection.

"We want revenge, vengeance, the perfect plan, retaliation, revenge, revenge."

Just as the friends are about to disperse, they hear an impressive racket. Harsh and impassive, the ambulance's siren disturbs the children, dogs and cats. No one stays in their room and none of them can understand a word. At last there is an audible shout: "I want to keep playing Golfin!"

"Detain him!"

"Where is the man who kicked me? I want the Dama who was my mirror!"

With everyone's intervention, they put Luciano into the ambulance, which frantically speeds away to the asylum.

"And… he was a good Golfin player."

AN EBONY NIGHT

"Who will loan me a slip…because…with this see-through skirt, my thighs—?"

"Look like deformed sticks!"

"Nosy! Nosy!"

"I'm not nosy. Inés Osorio, owner of the scandalous thighs, now, if you want…I'll loan you mine. That's the way: I am detached generosity!"

"Thanks, Generosity! I'll hold on to mine: fine, long sleepy roads, not your funeral meal of yuccas, mediocre malangas and smoked sausages—maybe you'll need them tonight!"

"Yuccas or gorgeous malangas, and those smoked sausages are really exquisite. And perhaps you'll need them today. Whichever ones I'm going to need, I don't think of it, I know how to manage my **devotees**—if you're saying that on account of my many admirers."

"It would be nice if they stopped fighting. Emilia, pass me the spray!"

"This one…!"

"No. The deodorant and everyone hurry up, because the dance starts at six."

"Which one of these do you want?"

"The feminine one!"

Laura's ensuite bathroom was not successful in protecting her from her busy friends' exchange of eyelashes, dresses and wigs—the more artificial they were, the more the more they will stand out at the party. To disentangle, discover, and locate an object or an instrument that produces beauty is not easy. The phrases sharpen and lengthen like afternoon rain shot thru with car horns—blaring and blaring spoiling the air, which is gravid with the poorly digested smoke from diesel vehicles.

The jumble in the room—dense with the fragrance of colognes, talcs, sprays—does not harmonize with the pretty dolls in glass cases, which are images of the saints from the village festivals.

They take turns scrutinizing themselves in the cloudy mirror while arguing quarreling and pushing. To the right of the gloomy mirror, a severely framed heart of Jesus ignores those possessed by a mix of passion and desire. Free from bras, their breasts beat in open solitary rebellion. Hundreds of invisible needles make their stomachs tense and their insides vibrate. Anxiety. Haste. The dance and the date. The encounter at the dance will culminate with kisses and morsels of words in their greedy ears and the audacious hands…At the dance, at the dance...The hands….

The lipstick disappears quickly as does the brightly colored rouge; pale, translucent foundation powder, and the brilliant shadows. The pressure on pressure, cheek to cheek to is done to achieve the right tone, the longed for charm.

On declaring themselves ready, they notice Laura has not left her improvised dressing room. When she does come out, the moment she brings up the disordered sprays, they deny it.

Inés and Emila, now reconciled, demand an explanation.

"They can go with you; I'm not going," Laura retorts in annoyance.

"Have I offended you by discussing this?"

"Hey, hey! What is this, huh?"

"Please, Emilia, Inés don't start again! But look...Look at Isela; what is…!"

Captivated by Laura's refusal, they had been ignoring the tears ruining Isela's elaborate make up.

"You want to tell us what the devil happened to them?"

An Ebony Night

Isela quickly replies, "To make my eyelashes shine…"

"…?"

"I used that container of Vasaline.…"

"That's VaporRub!"

"Now I know!"

They smile compassionately, interrupting themselves to surround Laura, who is undressing.

"And what are you doing?"

"I'm going to take a shower!"

"A shower? You…you're ready and ravishing, precious!"

"I want water and there isn't a single drop in this damned house."

"Water that burns Laura!"

"Stop it!"

"Don't be like that, lovely Laura, little Laura, the most Laura of Lauras, the greatest Laura, we want to cheer you up. Tell us, what do you want the water for?"

"For my ardor!"

"Ardor…where?"

"On my…pubis! I confused the sprays while you were bickering so marvelously."

Emilia and Inés laugh and laugh without temperance and Laura has to throw them out of the room.

For the lack of portable water, a bottle of Güitig mineral water without gas, very well administered will do. Laura frees her pubis from its ardor and helps Isela with her make up. Between the two of them, they tidy up the apartment.

On the bed, they chat cheerfully over a plate of small-grained corn.

"Isela, why aren't you dressing up and rushing to the dance?"

"If they see me with red eyes, they won't believe that it was from VapoRub, but from a fight with Panchín."

"Definitely?"

"Yes."

"You won't regret it?"

"Never."

"I believed you loved each other."

"We do love each other."

"If you don't explain, I—"

"It was because of his jealousy!"

"I don't believe you!"

"If I greet someone, he interrogates! If I look, he interrogates! If I smile, he interrogates! It's maddening!"

"And after two years of—"

"I've heard talk about the miracle of love. They just say that to excite the apathetic. The trees bear fruit. The avaricious become generous. It renews life. The birds sing. I include myself in the list! His jealousy would stop with love. I made a mistake. His jealousy increased and he started treating me like a pleasing object for a vain mind."

"You still love him?"

"And what of it? It's all the same if he had finished killing it or if I had turned into a woman like Mama who does not love my Father. Nonetheless, she carefully prepares his food, satisfies his needs and submissively tolerates his whims with patience. My brother and I are her horizon of tenderness."

"Does she suffer?"

"She lives resigned."

"Does he hit her?"

"We won't allow it!"

"Does he insult her?"

"No."

"What is it you're complaining about, then?"

"I don't know how long it has been since I caught her crying; with a handkerchief in her mouth so she wouldn't create a scandal. She recovered when she saw me, and a different image emerged out of her distressed expression. I talked about this and that without rhyme or reason. I dissimulated, but…I have never caught her crying again! She's enslaved by an allowance, which obliges her to sharpen her domestic talents. She hangs on a voice that thunders, whispers or decides. By his innate vocation as a leader, my father is the **loving patriarch**."

"What barbarity!"

"Mama was a linnet who cooed at my cradle. When I am all alone, I ask myself who stifled my linnet's voice and deprived my brother of its trills? Nothing hinders her from polishing her appearance and brushing her hair. If she smiles, her dark eyes sparkle. Disconcerted, Papa scrutinizes her gaze….No one knows if those dark eyes hide a lover who writes to her and dreams of her or about the special dishes she gives Papa. The man, who is irritated by everything and nothing, also squirms and vociferates due to his persistent stomach ulcer. Meanwhile my mother's mysterious eyes shine like immense stars lost in an ebony night."

PACHOCHA

The air on his face is exhilarating; he looks at himself in the mirror and presses the accelerator. He will control the minutes, he will conquer all of the kilometers, until he arrives. Arrives where? He has a Cadillac and he is racing along the roads in a Cadillac! He has a Cadillac and he is racing, racing, racing!

His destiny is to race; as a boy, he did it on a splendid bicycle.

The kilometers and minutes follow one after the other. The fine black needle leaps to eighty. Eighty, eighty! However, he could go to one hundred. The alignment and balance of the front tires is perfect. The engine is magnificent.

The bicycle was not his, but his friend Federico's.

To one hundred and twenty! No one would dispute that he is a great racer, and perhaps next year he will get to participate in that fantastic competition.

It had been a present from a suitor of his mother, a sensual widow. For that he detested her and because....

He must obtain a fast bird so he can have a co-pilot! And…bah, bah, he cannot go alone—without a co-pilot and win!

He preferred chasing butterflies around the pond at school, or slipping away to the city's wide river.

He is always imagining his domain, his power to drive. That majestic air, practiced so many times in the repair shop, would transform into reality. He feels that, since he owns the Cadillac, he also owns the highways, the trees and the avenues.

Federico never understood the pleasure his friend experienced when he raced and raced on his bicycle, sweating, thirsty and covered in dust.

His eyes devour the images that rush in to take him, but…recede. They recede violently and, after he passes by them, they bow reverently.

Federico loves the sun, the rain, the water. He dreams while taking in the fresh air, happy as the breeze, feeling it as intensely as his blood, penetrating his world, traveling his routes, reliving his stories…

The main road is a languid, slender young woman open to love. Love, love; he had never had time for it … only once when he was a boy, but his dreams soon shifted. He wanted a car, an automobile, a van. He had not dreamt that it would be so extravagant, brilliant, perfect, eternal.

…he knows the dark roots in depths of his bowels where dreams and love songs stir. On the white nights, he contemplates the jubilation of the sea, the fullness of the moon, the dance of the fishes.

Graceful and elegant, the black ballerina lifts herself to one hundred and thirty. The air flies past, the sun flies past, the birds fly past. Angered, the land looms in front of him. The driver is more adroit, and in time, he leaves it behind ridiculed.

The wind hangs from his tousled hair, it bites his face, it penetrates his lungs; his chest expands. How long has he been driving? Ignore space, dimension and time! His destiny is to race, race, and race!

He should be ashamed to recall it: four couples and a stolen car! They cast it to chance!

Federico, the boy-man, who embellished his life, decided to die when faced by an asthmatic priest, and his mother's renewal of an archived promise. In that way, serene and simple, he departed with the waters of the river he loved.

My girlfriend beside me and I hardly knew how to hold the steering wheel. All of my friends said, 'Although it is stolen, it cost silver, Pachocha. You know a lot of history, too much geography, but about this ….' The scoundrels laughed and laughed. I kept away from them. Better still, they kept away from me. Federico despised them and I…I used to go along with them.

Yes, this is driving. If only those rogues could see me…. This is racing. Racing. Racing. Racing.

The air flies past, the sun flies past, the clouds fly past, the birds fly past. Everything flies, flies and flies; in the meantime, he races faster, faster, and a little faster still.

There is a curve in the road and his brain clouds over, he confuses his feet and hits the brakes. The tires skid and he loses control of the steering wheel. Unrestrained, the tires swiftly turn and turn! There are screams, cries that deafen, that sicken!

The restless air, rarefied with the stench of burnt rubber, trembles under the ardent sun. On the ground a stain grows, a murmur rises. The stain, the stain spills over itself, the murmur stops.

His chest is sunken under tin, twisted iron, and shattered glass. Covered in dirt, his face is extremely pale. The wind continues to toy with his hair. A suave boyish smiles springs out on his lips, flecked with blood.

Pachocha, Pachocha, the friend of the neighborhood, the future race car driver who renounced college in order to be near cars, has died in a Cadillac, which he won in a raffle! Raffle, privations and the daily ingenuity for three meals!

The authorities and experts stand next to the mangled body, and say, "Excessive speed." They draw a little closer. Their faces look long and blank, and hastily they repeat, "Yes, excessive speed!"

NEW LILIANAS

"Whoever knows Mariela can't stop loving her!" She is willful, happy and dedicated to improving the appearance of our modest rooms. A piece of furniture never stays in the same pre-determined place very long before she is impelled to give it a prominent location.

"How pretty this sofa would be here. Yes. The living room looks like a mansion. But then…this little table, this little table… I would move it over there. No, no! All right, all right, we'll see…"

She would interrupt her work when you summoned her. A friend, stranger, acquaintance, or neighbor might be calling at your door, looking for thin, smiling, indefatigable Mariela.

"Mariela, please come here immediately."

Uninterested in prejudices, lacking in duplicity, Mariela will run in solicitously. She gives up her time and offers her care with the gentleness of a lark and the tenderness of a mother.

"Mariela, how can you be Liliana's friend when she abandoned her husband and her children?"

"Don't repeat that!"

"But if—"

"Quiet, woman!"

"There are those who say that—"

"Leave them to say it, but don't you form opinions about the things you don't know about."

"Perhaps you know something more?"

"No and if I did, I wouldn't tell you anyway."

"And why not, so that we can see?"

"Suffering deserves respect. I always will defer to the criminal rather than assume the role of the judge."

"A world without judges, where no one is going to stop, my god!"

"The best of all places!"

"You are strange and different Mariela."

"Join me. Be sensible to everyone's pain without caring about their trifles."

"Mariela!"

"Listen Andrea and don't foster more gossip. Liliana is not the monster that you think she is, but an unlucky woman."

"Her husband loves her."

"And he tortures, flatters, pampers, and offends her."

"Do you want to say that he beats her?"

"He beats her, he beats her! The physical pain passes, she forgets it. But she never forgets the cruel phrases!"

"I…I didn't know that."

"On one occasion he locked her in the bathroom, cut off the water, and disconnected the light. Liliana thought she was crazy and cried silently. By listening to the faint noises that came to her, she was conscious of the time passing. The girls must have already gone to sleep without dinner, since in order for them to have it, they needed to resort to her maternal ingenuity.

"'This spoon of soup,' the girls hated it, 'is for your dear father so he will bring a beautiful dress when he finds out that his little daughter ate it all. Eat this delicious piece of meat for your mama and you will see what a beautiful little story I'll make up for you.'

"Short nervous steps pause close to the door. Who has entered the house?

"'Don't leave me without light, light! And the door...don't lock me in! Hey, I'm in here; don't lock the dooooorr!'"

She resists believing her husband is capable of playing such jokes, but...no one else is able to do this to her... If she has gone crazy, crazy, then what about the girls? Crazy! No. Not crazy! She cannot be crazy. But, what do you do there on the other side of the door? I hear him breathing... When we married, he made a lot of drinks. I didn't want to...but he insisted. I never knew how we arrived at that place. I was lying down on soft refreshing grass with my naked body illuminated by the splendid moon. I sat up with a start, it didn't matter that he was kissing my feet. He was excessively gentle and horribly affectionate as he covered my body with some blankets. And I must share all the days of my life with this man. Once we were in the house, he put me on bed and left with that walk of his which is so precipitous and brief, without saying a word to me. When I was dressing, I noticed two things: I was intact, only...with my pubis shaved. A week later he came to my bed and offered an explanation for what had happened: 'I had to do it in order to save myself.'

The memory of that event inexplicably fills her with fear. She wants to pray, to say a prayer. She shakes her memory, pokes her brain, and only finds an endless space.

"Let's see Chelita, I know you can chew very well, who wants to teach your blonde doll that still hasn't learned how? Ah-ha, very good! Yes, yes...that's the way to chew! Chew over everything gently—without rushing: as if it is a piece of chicken gum, eh. I have two pieces here and I offer to give them to you if you eat everything right now."

A dull knock opens the door; the air attenuates around Liliana's swift escape. Since her eyes are accustomed to the darkness, they flood from the impact of the light from the flashlight. Her blood jumps, she has the impression that he is leaving.

"Would you like to leave life with me?"

"Only if I could die with my daughters."

Her husband waits for her with open arms and a sweet, serene expression on his face. "Darling, are you afraid?"

Liliana is perplexed. "Is this my husband's voice? Then I am crazy!"

When I woke up covered with flowers and loaded with kisses, I had no clear idea about what would happen next.

"Little woman, what happened to you? Are you sick? I didn't want to frighten you. After I came home, I knew you were in the bathroom. While I was waiting impatiently for your kiss, I decided that soothes me to play with you. Who else could I do it to, my little life?"

Liliana was not listening, she was not seeing, she went with the rising air in a hurry. Her kite was not pretty, but it rose.

"They ought to kill that man, Mariela."

"You're bloodthirsty!"

"Must I think that he is a lunatic?"

"But she's alone now, without cares, without love…poor thing!"

"I don't understand you Mariela. Tell me, do you think it is bad for a woman to leave?"

"No! There are others who are called to undertake that task."

"And what about her?"

"There is a man who would love having someone like Liliana to be by his side."

"And what about the girls?"

"They can make new Lilianas. And now you see Andrea. I must move my bed to another place."

THE TREASURE

Casilda's strange figure is accentuated by the discolored shawl which protects her head and arms, and by her threadbare skirt. Her rough bronzed shiny skin is speckled with dirt. Only her small brilliant eyes give life to the face hardened by her daily journey.

She lives alone, and it is well known that there is not a house where she has not done jobs, such as plucking turkeys, scrubbing floors, or washing dogs. However, this does not prevent the residents from circulating various rumors about her life and miracles.

"No one knows, girl. They've told me Casilda has trouble with a brother, and that ..."

"Micaela, what are you saying?"

"The pure truth, my girl; only what they wouldn't like you to hear."

Casilda is not ignorant of their gossip, but it does not seem to be important to her.

"Listen, neighbor, what does Casilda do with the silver she earns?"

"Just between us, Petronila, it seems to me that she gives it to a man, or the devil."

"It must be a man, neighbor, because the demons surely aren't seen anywhere, not even in statues."

"True, Petronila, true!"

And so, between stories about her work and other gossip, Casilda's life transpires, always someone else's, always a distant memory. How had she arrived in the neighborhood? No one knows. No one knows anything about this eccentric creature whose only pleasure consists in accumulating more and more money. They have never seen her laugh or cry, or barely talk.

All of a sudden she stops working for other women, even though they continue to ask her. The only house she continues visiting is that of Virginia Villa de Rosales. It is perhaps because Casilda discovered in her a little affection, or perhaps because both of them are used to living in eternal solitude.

Casilda's new position not only agitates the rumors, but also spreads stories of the intrigue throughout the entire neighborhood.

"Simonita, what did you find out last night?"

"I saw it myself with my very own eyes. Heaven help me. Who would have believed it? Casilda is adopting Lady Virginia's friends."

The neighborhood knows it. The gossipers have seen it. Everyone is sure. Casilda is receiving a man at night.

Without a friend, without a relative to close her large sad eyes, Virginia is about to die, and with her will die the mystery of her sadness and seclusion. Only Casilda, nodding off in the corner of the spacious bedroom, stays with her.

And when Virginia feels that death is about to take her, she says, "Casilda, come here. Bring me that coffer."

She holds it to her lips, and then says, "This is not meant for other eyes, Casilda. I can't destroy it. I want it to endure ... forever. It's a treasure ... my treasure."

And then her head lolls on the pillow that Casilda has so solicitously arranged. Her delicate profile is accentuated by the rigidity of death, and her large black eyes, now serenely sleeping, are no longer in harmony with her small fleshy mouth which still holds a breath of life.

Surprised and frightened, Casilda takes the coffer and leaves to hide it in her own house.

The following day, the great lady is buried with all the honors befitting a widow of a General of the Republic. The door of her house remains shut, and is sealed with a document bearing a long inscription.

Casilda is never able to comprehend why they did this. She only knows that she is in possession of a treasure. But what type of treasure? It is not jewelry or money. What treasure would hide in so many papers? If only she could read, she would know this very instant. Mistress Virginia kissed these papers. Why? Why? Oh, my God. Maybe white treasure exists? Tre-a-sures. Yes, treasure! Gold! Black gold; they say there's green gold! But, white gold? Is it possible that these are the papers which are rumored to be exchangeable for silver? She would have asked, but the dead woman had forbidden that anyone see these papers, her treasure, as she called them.

The dead woman's words and the papers' imperturbable silence do not leave her in peace, until she goes in search of the oldest and most wizened of her senior patrons.

"Don Alfonso...this...I...I want you to teach me to read." She lowers her head while rubbing her feet together. "I have a little money that I've saved over the years."

The old man looks at her affably. "Come to my house each evening. It won't cost you anything, daughter."

Casilda is desperate because she is unable to engrave the difficult characters into her dull memory.

If I don't learn, how will I be able to recognize that treasure? How, how!

Through drowsiness and fatigue, she slowly repeats, "A-A-A-A...C-C-C...A-A-A...B-B-B...C-C-C."

However, after three long months of repeating the difficult letters, she is discovering that she can join them to form words. And then finally, she is able to read them. The moment to decipher the treasure has arrived!

With trembling hands, she begins to explore the white treasure: pages and pages, so many! Which one should I start with? If only they were numbered. Let's see, what does this one say? No, not this one, no! Yes, that one. It's much smaller, and this one is very bulky.

She is bent over the small coffer, folding and unfolding the papers with her clumsy anxious fingers. Before she begins to read, she pretends to divine their contents.

Finally she opens the one that she had set aside, and begins reading slowly and with difficulty:

> 'Virginia,
>
> Why do you write me? I almost said: Why do you love me? I don't deserve so much love from you, if I, in exchange, together with my love as great as yours, also offer you so much sadness. The memory of me is an evil omen in your life. Oh, poor useless man! What is this pure, sacred, vehement love worth if I only give you pain?
>
> Pablo'.

Letting the paper fall, she interrupts the reading as her mouth blossoms into an expression of extreme disgust. To her, it is beyond a doubt: Mistress Virginia was crazy when she told her about the coffer and her treasure.

And for this, I learned to read, for this? She violently clenches her hands into fists and punches the air. After a few more minutes, she seems to contemplate which letter she ought to take next. She decides on the one whose letters she could barely see.

> 'My Friend,
>
> I am despairing for many things I have done. Your sorrow is my greatest punishment. I hurt as much as Guatemala, like a humiliated man: my private life circumscribed by a multitude of insurmountable barriers. You were made for me, not only to enlighten me, but also to receive the blessing for me. And I only give you solitude and grief.

Pablo.'

Tired by her futile effort, she does not want to continue reading. But, what if there's something in these letters which mentions the treasure? Then the best thing is to read everything, everything.

'My Beloved,

It is with sadness that I have known how your kindnesses have been returned in vain. Oh, your warm heart! Oh, your fountain of life, of tenderness and love! Today it is dry and I wither. I will no longer have your honeyed caresses that I so desperately desire: the purity of your voice, the freshness of your lips.

Pablo.'

'My Friend and Companion,

Why was life treating us that way? Ah, how weak I feel when I see you from far away! And I, I alone, alone with my tenderness without refuge, with my blood rebelling in my veins, my lips abandoned by yours, my hands without your body.

Pablo.'

She feels a strange turbulence in her solitude. It is her heart blooming as she reads the letters. And now, without thinking about searching for the treasure, she continues to read and thinks about the man who would have written these letters.

> 'My Darling Beloved,
>
> Do you, by chance think of me? Yes, I know you think of me, because I have felt your suffering and wailing in the distance. That man did not know how to cover you with kisses of tenderness, of love…First their uniforms, their soldiers, their empty speeches, and afterwards you, my love. Yes, My Love! Although in the eyes of the world, you may be the General's wife.
>
> Pablo'.

> 'Sweetheart,
>
> Here I am, your admirer, your tormented Argonaut. Estranged, sleepless, hypercritical, the two of us ask: Why is there so much pain in our immense love?
>
> Pablo'.

When Casilda finishes reading, she does know what is happening in her soul. She puts the letters away in the tiny coffer and kisses it tenderly the same way Virginia had done, without knowing why.

That night she sleeps the way children usually do: with a smile on her lips and a new, yet unknown joy in her heart.

THE SECRET

The moment Gustavo opens the bedroom door, he hears through the half-opened bedroom window the sound of the clock from the nearby church striking five o'clock in the morning.

He stumbles into the dark room. The sound of Lucia's serene breathing calms him. Without intending to turn on the light, he starts pacing from one side of the room to the other; but quickly stops when he hears a faint murmur. He approaches the bed; Lucia moves restlessly between the sheets. He turns on the light, and then he can see Lucia's contorted face.

The attacks have returned, thinks Gustavo. With a shudder, he recalls the dialog with the physician:

"Yes, Gustavo, I have to tell you the truth. Your wife will not survive another attack. You know, her heart...."

"No, doctor, save her...save her. She must live...please save her."

He grabs a few of the pillows, puts them under Lucia's head, and prepares to go out in search of the doctor; but a small and languid voice stops him.

"Gustavo...Gu-sta-vo." The woman speaks between anguished sobs. "Don't go away, and forgive me. Forgive me, for that also makes you...God." Before he can respond, she says these terrible words, "Gus-ta-vito is not your son."

He remains mute and motionless for a few moments. "Lucia, what did you say? Repeat it! Lucia...Luciaaaaaa!"

Gustavo's hands want to give life to that chest, a voice to that mouth; but his efforts are in vain.

His wife, that ingenuous and delightful girl whom he had taken for his wife, finishes her life by confessing her secret to him. "Gustavito is not your son."

It is impossible to yank the cruel confession out of his brain. *With whom? How? When was it? It was four years ago—that's the boy's age! But...do I know him? Is it one of my friends? Oh, if only I knew who it was!*

Panting, he rises from the bed where he fell conquered by the secret he must hide. *Hide it? And who knows the secret? Perhaps, the boy's father knows it? The father...but who is he? Who? Who? Who?*

With his eyes wide open, he approaches Lucia.

"Tell me. Who is it? Tell me who, tell me who, or I...."

His fingers convulse around her lifeless neck. *There's no longer anything I can do to her.* Ashamed, he withdraws and dries the rivulets of cold sweat on his forehead with his shaky hands. *I must keep quiet at the wake...at the burial...be quiet. I will observe...observe the face of each man. It's possible that he will come. He? Ah, yes...him!*

Somber and worried, he leaves the room. He has to arrange everything for the wake and the funeral.

Once he reaches the street, he begins to walk quickly.

He has to come. I will be able to recognize him. Did I say, 'I will recognize him'? He tries to smile, but he only manages to outline of a bitter expression around his mouth.

Two hours later, everything is ready. The small living room is full of chairs. In one corner the resplendent black box contrasts with the intense pallor of the corpse it holds. *She's still beautiful: the same as she was before. Even after death, even after her secret....*

Sitting in a corner, he spies on each guest's smallest movement, but he sees nothing. He does not detect a gesture or a revealing look.

He stands up quickly. He wants to walk, and yet he cannot take a single step. His face displays a deep anguish: his hands tremble. Slowly, he begins to walk like a boy trying his first steps. When he passes close to a group of people, he hears their comments. An obese lady, who is a chatterbox, stands facing him, looks at him, and then smiles.

She's laughing at me. She knows the secret. Secret? Bah!

He keeps walking. Before he leaves the living room, an elderly woman embraces him and says, "I'm very sorry, Gustavo. But you still have your son ... he's your living portrait."

"No! No!" he shouts in an injured voice.

"We understand, son. You resist accepting that you have lost her."

With a brusque motion, he moves away from the elderly woman. *Does that woman know something?* He continues walking. Suddenly he trips over something soft that forces him to stop; it is his son's little rubber rabbit.

My son. My son will help me. Yes, my son.

"But what about the father?" he speaks aloud. At the same moment he finds himself surrounded by curious people. The instant he realizes his stupidity, Gustavo falls silent.

"Poor man, he loved her so much."

"How he suffers!"

"It will be difficult to console him."

"They were a perfect couple."

They repeat the same comments in the living room and those terrible words reverberate in his head: "Forgive me, Gustavo. Gustavito is not your son...."

It isn't true, she lied. She was delirious. She lied in order to torment me. The boy is mine, only mine. She lied...

"She was crazy...crazyyyyy!"

After his scream with a horribly deranged expression on his face, he is speechless. Some of the men take him out of the room.

When he awakes, he has the sensation of having slept a lot. He has a headache. However, he reconstructs the scene, and immediately jumps out of bed.

There's no one here. I'm alone, but what about the boy?

The Secret   139

"My son!" The phrase burns his lips, and an invisible claw seizes his throat.

What a destiny. I lived for her. I worked for her. How did it help me? And I believed my line would be continued eternally.... He's her son, hers and I don't know whose! Who knows?

She had lain on the bed with her eyes closed. The images Gustavo sees of Lucia grow larger and larger. *Why did you tell me? Why? I wish you had remained silent forever. You were about to die and have your faults weighed before your god. Egotist, coward!*

He rises heavily from the bed with difficulty. He puts on some clothes and goes to look for the boy.

As soon as he sees Gustavo, Gustavito throws his arms around his father's neck, yelling, "My Papa, my Papa!"

"My handsome son." *My son? Why not? Perhaps our sons are not only those who carry our blood? There are also sons of the spirit...of pain....*

With his son in his arms, Gustavo begins to walk.

'My condolences, young man, you still have your son who is your living portrait.' No one asked you if he was your son, Gustavo. *'He seems so much like you....' 'We will call him Gustavo, like his Papa.'*

"Yeah, yeah, yeah, like Papa. Who said, 'like Papa'? She, she said it—"

"What are you saying, dear Papa?"

His crystal clear voice restores the peace. "Nothing, my son, nothing."

Yes, he's my son, the son of my love!

And father and son, who are joined in a single embrace, are bound for life.

PROFESSIONAL CONSCIENCE

It is a hot noon, stifling with the bustle of the city. Two men walk indolently down the street. Occasionally they stop, exchange words, and then continue on.

Both are young men. Alfonso has not yet completed his twentieth year. He has small eyes with a frightened expression similar to that of a rat in flight. His face is long, and a few bristly little hairs which stand out on his pronounced chin, win him the nickname 'Chivo'.

Guillermo, with his twenty-five years, is energetic and audacious. His pride is a fine chestnut-colored mustache. He has shiny gold teeth and a formidable body. His serene grey-green eyes reveal the effects of endless nights of insomnia. Hence they call him 'Gato Jumo'.

They dress very carefully, but in an extravagant fashion. Large chains, with small medallions depicting the Virgin Fatima, hang from their necks.

They stop on a corner to catch the bus, at a place where there is barely enough room not to suffocate in the amalgam of different smells.

Nevertheless, the young conductor insists, "Move forward, step to the back. The bus is empty."

But no one can move between the compact heterogeneous mass; except for Alfonso and Guillermo, who find the strategic ways through.

"Don't push!" a fading soprano voice suddenly yells.

"How dare you! Don't lean on me!" grumbles a plump woman.

"But, gorgeous, what do you expect me to do if they push me?" Guillermo replies nearly in her ear, and he leans even closer, attracted by that hot continent which sets all his pores boiling.

"Let me out, let me out!" shrieks an anguished little boy who carries a piece of dripping food between his fingers.

The agitated crowd changes size and shape every instant, but the friends who continue standing do not seem to have a set course.

A woman with a small turned-up nose, myopic eyes and a languid figure, protests, "It's sheer barbarity how you ended up ruining my stockings with your basket!"

"Listen here, you pestle, what are you doing? Who do you take me for?"

"Blah, blah, boss man—what's the matter with you?"

"What's the matter with me? What insolence! I should have you arrested."

"Get off!" a man shouts.

Guillermo timidly opens a path through the multitude. As he leaves, he says, "Look at that presumptuous woman, I barely grazed her."

Those who were near the lady comment, but the others do not have time to inquire. The bus continues on its way. Everyone is oblivious and indifferent until someone shouts, "Driver stop! Stop driver! I've been robbed ...my wallet....Driver."

"Wait until we get to the station."

A man with a square chin and a hardened face protests threateningly, "You have to stop."

"And will you pay us the fine for the delay?"

Without succeeding in halting the vehicle, they arrive at the station.

Then a weeping woman approaches the control room. "Do me justice, Sir. They just robbed me of my wallet...with money, other people's money, Sir."

Soon a group of curious spectators surrounds the elderly woman who is complaining. The supervisor looks at them through narrowed eyes and scratches his head while frowning. Later he returns to see her.

Professional Conscience

"But Ma'am, there's nothing I can do. You should have recovered it the moment they robbed you."

"Have pity, that money isn't mine, Sir."

"The only thing I can do—" He interrupts himself to talk to a little boy. "Listen, go tell the conductor named 'Pepito' to come here. It's so he can meet the driver," he explains to the woman. "But I don't promise you anything. Now go, and tomorrow at ten o'clock, present yourselves to the Transit Commission to see what they say there."

Δ

"Why did you take so long, Chivo? And how did you do? They made me so angry I could have roared."

"Well, I didn't feel that way. They didn't even realize the moment I acted. Now we'll see how much wool there is...."

They enter a restaurant, and as one keeps all of the sections under surveillance while continuing to cast darting looks at his friend, the other makes a prolonged search of the wallet. After doing a quick calculation and smiling with his little bulging eyes, Alfonso says, "We have enough for some days, Gato."

"Great, great! Then, hey waiter," Guillermo calls, clapping his hands, "beer and food for these customers." Once the waiter leaves, he adds, "Listen, listen Chivo, just to satisfy my curiosity...who did you nab, the peasant woman or the little boy?"

Pale and tremulous, Alfonso remains silent.

"Oooohh, sorry Chivo. I put my foot in it."

"Enough! Enough!" Alfonso jumps to his feet as he speaks angrily to his friend. "No, it wasn't the peasant or the little boy, you imbecile. Why do you have to remind me of this? Answer me, dammit! Why?" He bends his head down to keep the wallet, which had fallen to the floor, in his sight. Without breaking his gaze, he adds, "I stole it. I robbed the old woman. Now she's crying, cursing me for being a bad son, a bad man, a thief!"

Professional Conscience

The elderly woman's sweet eyes and threadbare blanket had reminded him of his mother. Then he had been a little boy longing to be a sailor, but one evening his mother left. The idea of living alone terrified him. He embarked upon his awkward turkey stage in a banana cart and left the land where the sad bones of his mother remained. These memories drew him to the elderly woman, but on seeing her voluminous wallet, barely supported under her frail arm, his professional conscience intervened.

Yes, yes. Didn't you go out for this? Coward, coward! What are you waiting for? Nabbing is your destiny, you know it! Nab it now; later it will be too late! These were the orders from his conscience, his professional conscience.

Barely able to contain the insistent throbbing in his chest, he smoothly slipped the wallet away, and then moved swiftly to conceal it inside his flamboyant sweater. He turned to his left, took a few steps backwards, and walked off the bus.

Now the fallen wallet reminds him of his skill in the profession. A proud smile appears on his lips. He glances at his friend, and then turns around to sit facing the table laden with food and liquor.

THE GHOST

I have always been intrigued by their very mismatched union: she young and beautiful; he a failed painter.

When I arrive, two friends are consoling her; I join them.

"Julia, you must calm down!"

With sad, widened eyes, she silently watches me. She seems not to understand.

I continue, "You have to rebuild your life, get used to being alone."

"Alone! Alone? No! I'm not alone. Something is growing and nourishing itself inside here." She holds her belly with her two hands.

Her reply leaves me surprised. (Previously I would have believed that it was the Koch bacteria that she contracted, those tiny beings that were the cause of Julia's widowhood.)

"But you knew that...?"

She regards me contemptuously and, responds in a haughty tone, "Yes, yes, I knew, because when I met him, he was already touched by death!" She pauses for a while so that she can then proceed more serenely. "His face was already marked; he had lost the brilliance of his black eyes. His figure was diminished from the loss of weight. Only his hands.... Did you see them sometime? Only his hands were full of life...the hands of an artist... powerful hands."

She stops abruptly. She examines her own hands as if for the first time. Then she brings them to her belly again; it is not yet swollen.

"Our son, Roberto, our son!" She suddenly screams and fixes her eyes on the place where moments before the overturned and lifeless figure of the man she loved had lain.

"Now, don't suffer anymore, Julia. Don't reminisce."

"Suffering! Remembering! That's it! That is the only thing I can do until my son arrives. And you won't be able to see him, Roberto. Now you'll never be able to see him."

Little by little, she regains her composure. Now her face looks like a clear sky after a long storm.

"Roberto loves you very much Julia, like his paintings."

She closes her eyes, tilts her head back and whispers very softly, "Yes, yes, life is only worthwhile when you have fulfilled your own destiny. See how I haven't forgotten it, Roberto? Neither have I forgotten our first meeting...."

Now with a vacant look, far away from her visitors, she begins to talk to Roberto, only to him. "I didn't know how to start until....

"Can I help you with something, Miss?'

"'I've heard the talk about your portraits with much enthusiasm, and I would like you to make one for me.' Only later did I understand how much you must have suffered when you heard from my profane lips the poor opinion they had for your art: for the art that you loved so much.

"Locked into painting an obscure piece, full of the pictures that your inexhaustible imagination produced incessantly, you saw the best years of your life vanish.

"Almost without looking at me, you said, 'We will start tomorrow, if you wish, Miss....'

"'Julia Mora, medical student.' My pride was talking; you made me feel so small.

"'Medicine…you must be a good student.' And you turned around to see me. That bite of rage was no longer in your voice. Now you regarded me in a different way.

"'I hope to be as good in my studies as you are in painting.'

"I can still hear how you answered: 'Please, Miss; I'm a beaten, defeated man. They have barely acknowledged me in my final hour, but that doesn't compensate for my dark life full of hopelessness and torture.

You're going to triumph, because triumph is your destiny. Yes, yes, I see it in your eyes, in your mouth. You will have to struggle, to suffer, but that is not important. Life is only worthwhile when you have fulfilled your own destiny. I ask you, I beg you; don't be discouraged, never, never.'

"Your voice vibrated through space, Roberto, and your eyes had acquired a fascinating brilliance. Since you wanted to calm yourself, you said, 'Everything is relative my friend, even triumph. It's not important, life is a struggle.'

"'And love,' I added almost unconsciously.

"'Yes…love.'

"And you gazed at me deeply. What a magnificent spirit there was in you, Roberto. No, you were not a beaten, defeated man; you refused to be so, even at the expense of yourself. For that, I loved you, and for your rebelliousness, and the faith that breathed in the ruined prison of your sick body. You have won, Roberto, because the triumph you yearned for is here; here inside me."

She remains silent for a few minutes; her spirit is already soothed by the communion she has with the beloved ghost.

Suddenly she notices us. "What are you doing here?" She shoots us a nebulous look, then cheers up to talk again with the living ghost: "Roberto…yes, my love, I already know that you haven't left."

"Julia, please. What's happening to you? Remember yourself."

"Silence, si-len-ce! Don't in-ter-rupt because Roberto is working on his paintings."

An ecstasy of love, of complete surrender, inundates her face. I am sure I see Roberto approach her and take her into his arms.

JACINTO

"Our son…his dreams!"

"His dreams, his dreams! And my dreams…what became of them? They were shattered!"

"No, they still exist."

"But they departed with him."

"They remain with us. They are claws that hurt, darts that wound."

"He went away, but something remains to—"

"Torture us."

"And we loved him so much!"

"Love, nameless, and soft."

"I spoiled him because I believed my little man would not live to run and jump as other children do. I began letting him have his own way, and it was beautiful to obey him, my beautiful son!"

"After all, he was created to show us our pride. I curse the instant! But I quit being that way; or was it after you contracted that vice?"

"Vice, you say? How is it that you can talk about vices? You, who glides like light foam over a prominent bust, or some rounded hips, or a firm pair of legs! You, who holds whatever woman who comes into your life in your arms! You converted love into a frivolous sport, because you gave it away like the pollen that blows in the breeze!"

"Shut up! Do not confuse the love between a male and a female with the disgusting practices between a pair of pestles."

"You are permanently chasing women. My little man believed in a spontaneous love. Everything must develop without rushing, without a schedule. Your machismo… 'Mother, if I vomit day after day, will I free myself from the ugliness that pounds through my veins?'"

"There is no doubt that you have lost your brain. Listen well; I say **'brain'** because sex with you is very frustrating. Do you know how hard it has been to share a bed with you when you are like an obstructive piece of furniture? Or a lifeless doll! Or a cadaver waiting for an autopsy?"

"Nooo. There was a time when I loved you and I wanted you so much that I counted the hours until your return, anxious to feel your arrival when you would envelope me with your aroma, where I trembled with the force of you rolling me onto your virile chest. I longed for your firm and gentle caressing hands, so tender and skillful! When I knew how many women could devour you, I stopped loving you; and, I suppose, I stopped desiring you too. You came to me and I thought about your sullied breath, your soiled root, your sweaty skin. And your messianic wisdom! It was fusion and feverishness, but fusion without soul! I felt dizzy and pushed away your arms, your farce of an impenitent lover killed my fire, the fire which I cultivated only for you. I silenced my blood when it lost your invigorating strength. What am I now? You said it: 'a cadaver waiting for an autopsy'. I am your first victim! Then…Jacinto, my son…went away—"

"On a journey! And this time he will return alone. Our Jacinto…alone, alone, a little sun…."

"I didn't want him to go!"

"His infancy had to be that way, without cruelty and pain. It will be better than mine. It will be dominated by air, Earth and sea. The women will indulge him, the elderly will tell him the way: 'Over there young man, just like we would have wished our son to be'. And I, only I, will be his father. Damned friends!"

"It was always for the best."

"It is not even important now that he has departed. His soul, his body, his blood all went with him."

"Our souls left with him."

"My favorite first-born; after the fiasco with Eunice and that damned foreigner."

"Our son!"

"He has been freed by his dearest friend, his best captain."

"Why don't they believe parents that have been driven crazy by the sea? So crazy that they bellow and rise up, jump, and wave? If you continue like this, I will only have to wait a little while for the burial; nevertheless…Jacinto, you enjoyed your fury; what a strange pleasure. It has been a while since I asked myself if I wouldn't have preferred for her body to roll with him."

"Eunice, why have you come here?"

"Wise judge, you forget that I am the universal heiress of your fire. Not even my mother submits herself like some languid lake. I love, I quiver, I live and it bothers me that you don't understand. And now, why don't you shut up? I don't think I will return to the house without Jacinto, unless I am dead; without Jacinto, it's horrible. You have Promethean egotism and jealousy, because I share my fire too. Do you want them to calcify my guts, and for me to grow wrinkled like some poor raisin? No, Mr. Judge! I came only for Jacinto! I want to tell you there is no issue between us, since people of excellent morals have already judged him. If those who request pardon when a belch escapes, or when they can't control the noise from their bowels, forget themselves, you reflect on Jesus; but in Jesus is the real truth, which always has love for the sorrowful. The great ministers of the world have lived your tragedy by loving the male and female molds with omission; basically in the normal position—horizontal. It is prohibited to remove all of one's clothes, the laws forbid it. They took my right to reform, to reject, to choose… My child, I straighten your sleeping lily and I walk without haste, so that your feet will not waver, nor will your chest tremble; and yet they still will not admit that they are also wounded people."

"Leave this instant, Eunice!"

"I hadn't thought of staying."

"Woman, you must rest a little…but, tell me…was it your womb perhaps? You had two children: that obstinate one and Jacinto who….!"

"I will not permit—"

"Why?"

"For love."

"Then…you were the bad soil…He was ten years old and you still bathed him!"

"My little blond, rosy-cheeked son!"

"A long time after he has departed, I will contemplate his sea; perhaps I will discover his smile or his shape behind the distant clouds. Many summers will pass. Autumn will follow autumn, and beautiful springs will strike my heart, but I will continue waiting! 'Father, I have impregnated tens of women, I've deflowered virgins by the heaps, I killed children in Vietnam…I raided banks, I have had to prove my strength, my valor …I did all of it, to…to please you!'"

"It was Jacinto's friend who stayed with me."

"In reality…there is little time left for a conclusion."

"Then…!"

"Humhnm, with you my wife won't feel lonely, as long as I return in a few seconds."

"He was my son's friend!"

"Also a little like his...student."

"Good heavens, my son's schoolmate?"

"Jacinto had the charming soul of a child. He was anxious for affection."

"He never lacked my affection!"

"What sort of dick is the world when, at the height of an unfinished journey, we depart one day without brilliance in our eyes or rhythm in our hearts!"

"That's life!"

"That's death! Even though life and death sustain and inspire us, I detest them."

"Are you a renegade? My son did believe."

"In what…ma'am?"

"In the Divine, in the beauty of a dead saint."

"I also believe in the god in your son."

"The one in my son is mine. I taught him how to pray and I took him to church."

"Our god is love. Ah, Jacinto, youth illuminated, a brimming fountain that a light breeze spilt over."

"When did you see each other?"

"It's been two days!"

"You don't find it strange?"

"I'm worried about something you don't want to tell me."

"His friends loved him and his father…I adored him. Why….?"

"Why wonder...if you glow with contentment? We used to talk about…he interrupted himself to tell me, 'They're over there, spying on us.'"

"Who would spy on you in your own house? I have to know who. Come with me!"

"You have to start again because I asked you to do it! I demand it of you, I order you, and because I will teach you how to be a man without that stupid pampering from your mother."

"No one knows anything, no one says anything."

"Enough!"

"My blond and rosy-cheeked baby has gone to sleep! Dolores, see that no one makes any noise! Turn off that radio, Dolores, my baby is sleeping. My child is sleeping, my Fine Gold Thread! He sleeps in my arms, he dreams his dreams. You are my precious treasure. Don't be sad or afraid, my Fine Gold Thread!"

"I fertilized the egg without the dreaming that—!"

"Dolores, hurry, my son wants his bath! Bring me the bathing salts and my rose-colored robe that he likes so much!"

Quick Order Form

Satisfaction guaranteed

Email orders: janeknows@gmail.com
Fax orders: (636) 333-8993. Send this form.
Phone orders: Call (415) 794-3268. Have your credit card ready.
Postal orders: Jane Knows Intellectual Property, Inc.,
PO Box 190142, San Francisco, CA 94119-0142, USA.

Please send the following books. I understand that I may return any of them for a full refund—for any reason, no questions asked:

_____

_____

Name: _____
Address: _____
City: _____ State/Province: _____
Country: _____ ZIP/Postal Code: _____-____
Telephone: _____ Fax:_____

Email address: _____

Sales tax: Please add 8.5% for products shipped to California addresses.

U.S.: $11.95 for the book and $5.00 shipping and handling.

International: $11.95 for the book; $8.80 shipping and handling. (Estimate)

Payment: ☐Check ☐PayPal accepted. For credit card orders please complete information below

☐Visa ☐MasterCard   ☐Discover ☐☐Optima ☐ ☐AMEX

Card number: _____
Name on card: _____Expiration date: ___/__

Thank you for your order!

Printed in Great Britain
by Amazon